STRANGLED IN SOHO

CASSIE COBURN MYSTERY #4

SAMANTHA SILVER

BLUEBERRY BOOKS PRESS

CHAPTER 1

I woke up to the sound of the familiar, rhythmic beeping of a heart rate monitor. One beep per second. Sixty beats per minute. The person lying in that hospital bed had a completely average resting heart rate.

It took me a moment before I realized that person was me.

I kept my eyes closed, as if I could slip away into sleep once more and awaken in my one-bedroom basement apartment under Mrs. Michael's house. It wasn't that I disliked hospitals. In fact, I'd spent a large portion of my life thinking I'd spend my entire working life in one. It was just that I didn't like waking up in them. I didn't exactly have great experiences with that.

Despite my closed eyes I could still hear the regular

beeps from the heart rate monitor. I supposed this was real life after all.

With a great effort, I forced my eyes open, and focused on the man sitting by the bed, concern etched on his face. As soon as he saw I was awake, he grabbed my hand.

"Cassie! Cassie, you're awake," he said. "Thank God!"

I was staring into brilliant blue eyes and shaggy blond hair that made Doctor Jake Edmunds look more like he belonged on a beach in Australia with a surfboard tucked under his arm than sitting by my side at a hospital in London.

"I'm not going to be one of your clients just yet," I replied weakly, just managing to crack a smile. Damn, my throat was dry. I looked around for some water, and Jake, as if he could read my mind, grabbed a cup off the nightstand and helped me take a sip. While Jake was a doctor, he didn't work at the hospital, he worked at the local morgue as a pathologist.

"Good," he replied.

"What happened, anyway?" I asked.

"What happened is that somewhere along the line, your evolutionary instincts to be aware of anything unfamiliar were overridden by your apparent inability to resist putting any food you come across into your mouth," came a reply in the form of a French accent, as Violet Despuis pulled aside the privacy curtain and stepped into the makeshift room as well.

She was a striking figure; tall with long, dark-brown hair tied back into a braid that ran down her back; today she was wearing high-waisted, galaxy-print leggings with an oversized black-and-white striped top.

Jake glared at her. "You can't seriously blame Cassie for this."

Violet shrugged. "Well, if she had not eaten the chocolate brownies I had left on the kitchen counter, then there would have been no problem."

I leaned back in my bed and groaned as my memory of what had led to me coming here was slowly starting to come back.

~

I'd gotten a text from Violet asking me to meet her at her house at ten in the morning. When I knocked on her front door, there was no answer, so I tried the handle and found it was unlocked, which I found quite frankly kind of alarming given the nature of Violet's work.

I called out to her and got a reply almost immediately from upstairs. "I will be down in a minute!"

Since I hadn't eaten breakfast yet, I made my way toward the kitchen, despite knowing that Violet and I had, uh, slightly different tastes in food. I figured at the very least I could find a banana or something. And yet, to my surprise, there was a plate full of brownies just sitting on the table. They'd obviously been freshly baked; the aroma of caramelized sugar and chocolate wafting toward me and making my mouth water.

I figured Violet wouldn't miss one little brownie. In fact, they were probably a gift; I couldn't imagine Violet cooking brownies to save her life, unless they were made with like, figs instead of chocolate or something equally high in vitamins and low in taste.

Still, even if she was my friend, it would be rude not to ask.

"Can I have a brownie?" I shouted up the stairs, but didn't get an answer. I could hear water running through the pipes; I assumed Violet was having a shower. My hunger won out over my rudeness—it wasn't like Violet was going to eat these brownies anyway, I knew her well enough to know she'd just scrunch her nose at them and eat an apple or something before offering them to me with a snide comment about my eating habits—and I reached over and grabbed one.

Sinking my teeth into the warm deliciousness, I quickly ate the brownie. I was pleasantly surprised to discover there were walnuts in the mix, and when I finished off the first brownie I quickly reached over and grabbed another.

Soon after finishing the second brownie, however, I began to feel dizzy. I grabbed the table to stabilize myself as I heard Violet making her way down the stairs. She came into the kitchen, still drying her long hair with a towel, which she immediately dropped as soon as she saw me.

"Cassie! Cassie! *Merde,* you have eaten one of the brownies, haven't you?" she asked, glancing at the plate. "Two of them! *Merde!* We must get you to the hospital right now!"

Violet pulling out her phone and calling for an ambulance was the last thing I remembered before falling to the floor, unconscious.

~

"What was in the brownies?" I asked, almost afraid of the answer.

"Belladonna," Violet answered matter-of-factly. Jake shook his head in disbelief next to me, grabbing my hand.

"But… there's no cure for that," I said. "Why aren't I dead?"

"Correction," Violet said. "There *was* no cure for it. You, Cassie Coburn, are the first person to ever overdose on Belladonna and survive."

"You left those brownies out for Cassie as a trap?" Jake asked, his face reddening as he got up from his chair.

"Of course not, do not be ridiculous," Violet replied, leaning casually back as she sat down in another chair herself. "I did not expect Cassie to eat brownies that were left out on *my* kitchen counter. I had made them in order to test both the antidote that I had developed, and in order to solve a case that I was working on."

"So, who was supposed to eat the brownies?" I asked.

"I was going to suffer through eating one myself, with you on hand as the doctor to supervise and to administer the antidote. That was why I had texted you to come to my house."

I grinned. "Really? *You* were going to eat something made with real sugar and butter? There were probably trans fats in those brownies!"

"You can mock my eating habits all you want, but you are the one sitting in a hospital bed because the allure of empty calories was so great you could not wait until I had finished my shower to ask if they were for you."

"Maybe you shouldn't leave poisoned brownies just sitting around in your kitchen, like a normal person!"

"Normal people do not single-handedly develop an antidote for the poison that murdered the Emperor Augustus of Rome and countless others since," Violet sniffed, evidently taking offense at my implication that she was anything remotely resembling normal. She did have a point, I was pretty sure there wasn't a single thing about Violet Despuis that could be considered normal. "Not to mention, I have now solved my case, and as we speak DCI Williams should be on his way to arrest a certain man who murdered his ex-girlfriend."

"I'm glad I was able to help," I said dryly. "Now, I'm starving, did you bother to make any brownies that you didn't lace with a deadly poison?"

Violet threw her hands up in the air. "You are *impossible*! How can you want more brownies after nearly dying?"

"I did ask for some without the poison," I replied.

Jake grinned and stood up. "I'll go get you some food. That pub you and Brianne like to hang out at is near here, right?"

"We're at the Royal London?"

"Yes," Jake nodded. "Violet decided it was going to take too long to get to Charring Cross Hospital during morning rush hour, so she called a friend and had him fly a helicopter over. He landed at that junction by the church at the end of the road, and they flew you straight here."

I smiled at my friend; despite the fact that she could be completely oblivious to the fact that normal people didn't leave poisoned brownies out on the kitchen table, I knew that calling in a favor and having a helicopter land at the end of the street to take me to the hospital was her way of showing she cared.

"The neighbors must have loved that," I grinned.

Violet shrugged. "It would not be the first time that they have grumbled about my actions. Mortimer Barlow came running after us when you were being loaded into the helicopter, shouting about how I was a nuisance and that my presence was ruining the reputation of the neighborhood, but luckily Mrs. Michaels came out–still in her dressing gown and curlers—and threatened to beat him to death with her rolling pin if he didn't go back into his home and let me get you to the hospital."

I burst out laughing at the thought of my octogenarian landlady chasing down Mortimer Barlow, an advertising executive who always looked like he'd spent the day sucking on a lemon. I had no doubt she would do it, too.

"What would you like from The White Hart then?" Jake asked.

"Oooh, I'd love a burger and fries," I said happily. "I'm not sure they do take-out though."

"Don't you worry about that," Jake said to me with a wink. "I find most places are happy enough to do take-away if you ask nicely enough."

"As long as there is a woman working, I would bet," Violet said, making Jake blush and me burst into laughter.

"Anyway," Jake said, "I'll be back soon. If they don't do take-away for me I'll get you Nando's. Sound good?"

"Sounds wonderful, thanks," I gushed, my mouth watering at the thought of food. I'd already been hungry when I ate the brownies, and I didn't know how much time had passed since, but I knew my stomach was growling.

STRANGLED IN SOHO | 9

Jake left and I looked at Violet.

"So tell me about this case that I've decided I was instrumental in helping solve." Violet smiled before leaning back in her chair and telling me the whole story.

CHAPTER 2

*A*bout ten minutes later Violet had finished telling me her story, and I was shaking my head in awe at the absolutely incredible deducing she had had to do to nail the ex-boyfriend. The brownies being poisoned with a specific amount of belladonna had in fact proven that he was the guilty party.

Suddenly, there was a commotion on the other side of the privacy curtain, to my right. I looked over to see the bottom of a bed being brought in next to mine, a couple pairs of legs in scrubs and crocs next to it.

"I want her monitored for cardiac arrhythmia," I heard a woman say, probably a doctor. Suddenly, a heart rate monitoring machine went nuts, emitting three quick loud beeps in a row. I knew that sound all too well; the patient was going into cardiac arrest.

"She's coding, get me some paddles," the doctor ordered, and the legs I could see rushed over toward the other side of the bed. A moment later the whirring sound of the paddles charging filled the air and the doctor cried out "clear!" a split second before the jolting sound of the paddles sending electricity shooting through the patient's chest sounded out.

I let out the breath I didn't realize I was holding as the frantic beeping stopped, replaced once again with the rhythmic sound of a regular heartbeat. My new neighbor had been stabilized.

"Right. I want someone checking on her every five minutes, tops. And the instant she wakes up, if she wakes up, I want someone at her side. We're dealing with a near-suicide here."

"I'll keep tabs on her, doctor," a man volunteered.

"Good," the doctor replied, and I heard her brisk footsteps continuing down the hall. Violet looked curiously toward the privacy curtain, and as the nurse who had offered to stay behind left, she got up from her chair and headed toward it.

"Violet," I hissed. "You can't go in there! You don't know who that is!"

"I just want to have a quick look," Violet replied.

"This isn't a zoo, it's a hospital."

"I am a scientist, I study human beings. I simply want to study what effects this person's attempt at suicide has had on them, physically."

"If you get yourself kicked out of the hospital, I'm not coming to your defense," I said, shaking my head. I knew there was no dissuading her.

"Fine, but do not forget that I had a man land a helicopter on Eldon Road in order to get you here faster."

"I only needed to go to the hospital because you're the one who poisoned me in the first place!" I exclaimed.

"I did not force you to eat the brownies."

Before I could reply, Violet slipped behind the privacy curtain; I let out a sigh and leaned back in the bed, closing my eyes, pretending that one of my best friends wasn't also the craziest person in the world.

About two minutes later Violet came back onto my side of the curtain, her face grim. She instantly pressed the button to call the nurse.

"What are you doing? I don't need a nurse."

"No, but she does," Violet said, pointing to the curtain.

Before I had a chance to ask what was wrong, a kindly looking woman in her fifties popped her head into the curtained area. "Someone called for a nurse?"

"Yes," Violet said. "You must call the police, immediately."

"Why? What's happened?"

"The woman in the next bed did not attempt to kill herself. Someone tried to kill her."

The silence that fell over the three of us as Violet's words sunk in was suddenly interrupted by another series of beeps as the heart rate monitor's alarm went off. The woman next door was crashing again.

"Stay here!" the nurse ordered as she rushed over to

the room next door. A moment later Jake walked in with a brown bag full of food, the aroma of cooked beef and oil wafting through the room as I reached eagerly for the bag.

"You're the best," I said as Jake came over and gave me a kiss before I reached in and pulled out a burger wrapped in foil and a pile of fries. The sound of the paddles charging next door made me pause; I hoped the woman was going to pull through.

"What's going on?" Jake asked, nodding his head next door.

"Someone tried to kill the woman in there, and made it look as though she hung herself," Violet said. "She is having a heart attack. She had another one perhaps five minutes ago; I do not need to be a doctor to know that things are not looking good for her."

I shook my head sadly, and breathed a sigh of relief when a moment later the woman's heart rate monitor began beeping normally once more. She'd been brought back from the brink yet again.

As I eagerly unwrapped the burger, the nurse poked her head back into my makeshift room. "Now, you said I needed to phone the police?"

~

Twenty minutes later I was happily munching away on a fry as I slowly worked on my burger, and a nurse who came by to check on me let me know that I'd likely be discharged early the next morning, they wanted to keep me overnight for observation. The head of the hospital wanted to speak with Violet about her development of an antidote against belladonna poisoning, and she promised to stop by when she got a chance.

A few minutes after the nurse left, a man dressed in a cheap, ill-fitting suit came into the room. He had a permanent snarl on his face, which was topped with a thin layer of greying hair, and gazed around at the three of us as if we were completely underneath him.

"Doctor Edmunds," he said. "Didn't expect to see you here among the living."

"DI Carlson," Jake replied, and I noticed the discomfort on his face. "The higher-ups sent you here to look at a potential murder, did they?"

"Well, I was the one called in when they found the body."

"She's not dead yet, calling her a body is a bit presumptuous."

"You doctors and your details. Point is, lady killed herself. Open and shut case. I don't know who here told the nurse to call the coppers, but it's a waste of time. Poor woman did this to herself."

"I am the one who had the police called," Violet said from her spot in the corner. Her voice was frosty; evidently she didn't like what she'd seen so far from DI Carlson. He turned to face her.

"And you are?"

"Violet Despuis," she replied.

"Ah, you're the meddling Frenchie who reckons herself a bit of an investigator, aren't you?" he asked.

"If by that you mean the woman who has uncovered the perpetrator of over two hundred and fifty crimes in London that the police were incapable of solving, then yes, that is me."

"Well, love, let me give you some advice," DI Carlson said, obviously talking down to her. Jake and I shared a glance; I had a feeling this conversation wasn't going to end well for DI Carlson. "I've been with the Metropolitan Police since you were in nappies. I was at the home. I saw where the woman had been hanging, and she definitely did this to herself. I know it's fun to think everything's a crime, and that you get a bit of attention here and there from people with the patience to humor you, but why don't you leave the detecting to the *real* detectives?"

"If you have such *extensive* experience with death, then how do you explain the location of the bruises on the woman's neck?"

"What do you mean?"

"It is obvious to anyone with a pair of eyes and a half-functioning brain! The bruising on her neck is consistent with a rope, but it is far too low, and the angle is all wrong! She was strangled with the rope pulled down behind her. I expect that if you were to look at her back you would find a bruise there as well; my guess is she was lying face down, and her would-be murderer pressed a knee into her back as he strangled her."

DI Carlson chuckled. "That is quite the vivid imagination you have there, Violet," he told her. "But I assure you, I've looked at the crime scene. The victim was found hanging from the ceiling fan in her home, and she left a suicide note. Why don't you leave the policing to the *real* police?"

Violet's eyes flashed with anger. "You have given me some advice, now let me give you some of my own," she said, standing. She wasn't exactly tall, but the commanding way in which she stood even made DI Carlson take a step back. "Understand one thing: I am much, *much* better at your job than you are. You are no more than a buffoon who has evidently been promoted once too often, and I will not let your inability to develop anything remotely resembling critical thought result in a murderer being allowed to roam free. Now, you are welcome to continue to wallow in the puddle of your own ignorance, but not to the detriment of law and order in this city. Accept that what I have told you is the truth, and treat this as a homicide that I can solve for you, or when I solve this attempted murder on my own, I will ensure that your name is dragged so far into the mud that the most important duty you will ever be given in the future is to ticket drunken students urinating on buildings in the middle of the night."

Damn. Violet was not playing around. DI Carlson's

face paled for a minute, then he found his voice once more.

"I know you think you're a pretty good *amateur* detective, but I know how you frogs work," he said. Seriously? People still used 'frog' as an insult against French people? "This is my case, and you stay away from it. There's nothing here. I don't want you going around sticking your nose in police business, pretending you're some hotshot who knows better than a twenty-two-year veteran of the force."

Violet shrugged and sat down. "Fine. Do not say that I did not warn you."

"Lady, if I find you interfering in my cases, you'll be sorry," he said, evidently upset that Violet hadn't taken his warning seriously. She laughed in reply.

"Oh, I am sorry," she said a moment later. "Was that supposed to be a threat?"

"It was," DI Carlson growled at her. "If you know what's good for you, stay out of this. It isn't a murder, and I don't want some foreigner going around making trouble for me. Now, I've had enough of this. I'm warning you: stay out of this."

And with that, DI Carlson stormed out of my makeshift room. Violet shook her head.

"I cannot stand people who are too lazy or stupid to do their job properly."

"You're sure it's attempted murder then?" Jake asked, and Violet simply gave him a *look*. "Ok, you're sure!" he said, raising his hands up in front of him.

"Do you know him, this DI Carlson?" Violet asked, and Jake nodded.

"As you've discovered for yourself, he isn't the sharpest tool in the shed. He's old-school, and uh, I suspect whoever called it in mentioned that it was a suicide, otherwise I imagine they would have at least put a Detective Chief Inspector on the case. Or anyone else, really."

"Well that is not promising."

"No, I can't say it is. If she ends up coming my way I can try and have her assigned to me; if I label it a homicide then the police will be forced to investigate."

"Thank you," Violet said to Jake.

"No problem. As much as your bedside manner could use some refining, you do tend to be right about these things."

"I am *always* right about these things," Violet corrected. "Besides, there is nothing wrong with my bedside manner."

"Opening with how much of an idiot the guy was probably didn't do you any favors."

"Fake flattery is pointless. It was obvious the woman had not tried to kill herself; I looked at her for maybe thirty seconds and I already knew that."

"Flattery is what got Cassie that burger that she's apparently trying to eat in a single bite," Jake said, grinning at me.

"Hey!" I tried to argue, but with my mouth full of

delicious cheeseburger, it came out as more of an angry grunt; I wasn't exactly painting myself in the best light.

"I do not do flattery, I do facts," Violet replied haughtily. "If the man was too ignorant to understand what I was saying to him, well, that is not my fault. At any rate, I now have an attempted murder to investigate, as it appears that if I do not do it, then no one else will."

CHAPTER 3

*J*ust after three-thirty that morning, I woke up to the sound of the woman next door's heart rate monitor alarm going off once more. I was groggy, but I still was able to register the sound of the paddles jolting the woman's heart one, two, three, four times before finally the monitor let out a single steady beep indicating a flatline.

The woman had died. My heart sank at the realization that Violet was now investigating a murder.

I fell back asleep soon afterwards, and by the time I woke up Violet was sitting in the chair, texting away.

"Ah, good, you are awake," Violet said. "Brianne will be here soon."

"I assume you saw your strangulation victim died last night?"

"I did," Violet nodded sadly. "It is too bad, if she had woken up and was able to tell us what had happened, it would have been an easy solution to the case. But of course, my hopes were not high when she crashed twice within twenty minutes."

"How do you know Brianne is coming? You don't have her number, do you?"

"I have hacked into the websites of government departments in the past, do you really think the password on your phone was going to stop me?"

"Figures," I muttered in reply. I wasn't exactly annoyed; I'd learned a while ago that password-protecting something wasn't enough to keep it from Violet. Brianne had come to visit me the night before, when her shift had started. A medical student from Australia, most of her practical work took place here at the Royal London Hospital.

"Cassie! Violet! Good morning!" Brianne said as she swept away the curtain and entered the room with a cheery smile. Brianne more than made up for her short stature by being huge in energy. I was pretty sure she was nearing the end of a ten-hour overnight shift, but that wasn't going to stop her.

"Good morning, Brianne," Violet said. "Thank you for not mentioning that visiting hours do not start for another two hours."

"Would it have made a difference if I had?" she drawled in her Australian accent, shooting Violet a grin.

"No, but it is polite of you all the same."

"Now, as much as I'm glad to see Cassie's doing all

right this morning, I figure you probably have something more important you want me to take care of?"

"Yes, please," Violet said. "I need you to find out everything you can about the woman who was in the bed next door, who died early this morning."

"Oh, that's so sad," Brianne said, shaking her head. "Her name was Amelia Waters, and apparently she hung herself."

"She did not hang herself," Violet said. "She was murdered."

"So that's why you want her information," Brianne nodded, understanding. "I suppose the police will be by shortly to get her things, then?"

"The policeman in charge of this case seems to have a lower IQ than the glass of water by Cassie's bed," Violet explained. "He is convinced that it is a suicide, whether out of laziness, stupidity, or some sort of grotesque combination of both I am not yet certain. But regardless, the police will not be by for her things, not soon, anyway. In so far as they believe–until the autopsy is complete–young Miss Waters killed herself."

"Yikes," Brianne said. "Ok, so you need the information since the police aren't going to care."

"Exactly."

"I'll see what I can do."

"Brianne?" I asked.

"Yeah?"

"Don't do anything that will actually get you into trouble," I warned. She flashed me a grin in reply and left, and I shook my head. Brianne was always happy to be involved in Violet's cases in whatever way she could, and I hoped it wouldn't get her in trouble with the university.

"When she gets back it'll be time for you to check out, seeing as you haven't died overnight," Violet said.

"Do I have time to eat breakfast first?"

About ten minutes later Brianne came rushing back into my makeshift room, carrying a big brown box full of clothes and other personal effects.

"This is all she had on her when she was brought in," Brianne explained. "Now, I have to get going, I'm not off shift yet. I'll be back to get this in about fifteen minutes; I don't think I can get away with explaining why it's missing for longer than that."

"Thank you, Brianne. You have been very helpful," Violet told her, and Brianne grinned.

"Anything I can do! Solving a murder sounds exciting!"

"Too exciting, a lot of the time," I said, and Brianne laughed as she left the room once more.

Violet pounced on the plain brown box like a cat having just found some prey.

Unfortunately, there wasn't too much information to be found in the box. The woman had been wearing a plain black skirt and a red blouse when she was found, both of which had been cut off her, along with a pair of plain black socks, and a matching set of lacy bra and panties. There was a watch as well, a mid-range one, engraved at the back. "Love you, duckie. Mum & Dad." She also had a pair of nice sapphire earrings, a pair of studs.

My heart immediately sank for the parents who were most likely receiving the worst news a parent can get; I wondered why they weren't already here. When they had called my mom in the middle of the night to tell her I was in the hospital, she'd apparently broken every traffic law on the books to make it to the emergency room in under twenty minutes.

Violet also pulled out a copy of the girl's intake form, which she passed over to me after looking at it. This definitely had more information on it. For one thing, the address where she was found was listed, in Soho.

"Soho... that's pretty expensive, isn't it?" I asked Violet, who nodded.

"Definitely. It is in West London, practically right in the city."

I read over the report quickly. It stated that the woman was found unresponsive by her flatmate, but that she still had a weak pulse. He immediately dialled 9-9-9, and the ambulance brought her here to the Royal London.

Apart from that, I hadn't learned anything else about Amelia Waters.

"Great," I said, putting the form back in the box. "That was kind of useless, apart from the home address."

"Oh, I would not quite say that," Violet said with a small smile.

"Even you couldn't get much out of this box, surely!" I exclaimed.

"It is true, it was not the most enlightening box of personal effects through which I have looked in hopes of gathering information, but it also was not useless. We now know that Amelia Waters lives in Soho, but that she is originally from the East Midlands, most likely Nottinghamshire. She does not come from a rich family, but most likely middle to upper-middle class. However, she does have a *very* rich boyfriend."

"Ok, I give up," I said. "How did you get all of that from what was in that box?"

"The address where she was found was listed on the intake form. It is in Soho, and nobody commits suicide outside of their own home, except possibly in a hotel room, and I know the address, it is a residential building. Even an amateur murderer would know not to kill his victim and string her up away from her home. The watch has an engraving on it, which shows she is from the East Midlands, where 'duckie' is commonly used as a term for affection."

"Well, at least I couldn't have known that one," I replied, feeling a little bit less like an idiot. After all, I'd only lived in London for six months, I could hardly be expected to master the linguistic individualities of all the regions of England.

"You also have not made observation your way of

life for the past twelve or so years," Violet said to me with a smile. "It would, quite frankly, reflect quite badly on me if you were able to detect everything as well as I have. Looking at her clothing, it is obvious that she did not come from a rich family, but not a poor one, either. The brands are decent–her skirt is Tommy Hilfiger and the blouse is from Ralph Lauren, so they cost a little bit, but not an extravagant amount. The clothes are of good quality, but they were also not a regular purchase; the skirt has been re-hemmed a couple of times, rather than thrown out and a new one purchased."

"But what about the rich boyfriend?" I asked.

"The earrings," Violet replied matter-of-factly.

"They are pretty nice," I said, picking them out of the box and looking at them once more. Even in the clinical fluorescent light of the hospital the jewels glittered.

"They are from Tiffany and cost nearly two thousand pounds."

I let out a yelp and tossed them back into the box, making Violet laugh. "Just because you have held them does not mean you have to pay for them."

I wasn't exactly struggling for money, not after a multi-million-dollar payout from the insurance company of the man who had hit me with his car and ended my career, but years of being raised by a single mom and trying to make my way through medical school with as little debt as possible meant that mentally, I was still pretty frugal.

"Two thousand *pounds*?" I asked, amazed. "Man, the guy must have *really* liked her."

Violet nodded. "Or, as is more likely, he was the kind of man for whom two thousand pounds was nothing. After all, it was likely a new relationship."

"You can't know that," I said, exasperated.

"He has bought her new earrings but not yet bought her new clothes? That is a sign of a relationship closer to infancy than long-term."

"Maybe they've broken up and she just kept the earrings," I suggested, but Violet shook her head.

"No, the earrings are from a new collection, and she would not be wearing them if the breakup was recent."

Everything Violet said made perfect sense. "So, let's go down to Soho and see if a man wearing a suit that costs more than my yearly rent answers the door," I replied.

"Good, then you are ready to leave the hospital," Violet said with a smile.

I hopped out of the bed and prepared myself for discharge while Violet gathered everything back into the box to give back to Brianne.

CHAPTER 4

*F*orty minutes later Violet and I were standing in front of Ted's Grooming Room, the barber shop at the street level of number 42 Berwick Street, the address to which the paramedics had been called to find Amelia Waters' body.

A convenience store on the corner had the day's main headlines in the window: "*The Terrible Trio Rob Diamond Shop*" was the main headline of The London Post-Tribune. Below it, however, The Sun had a different headline: "*Media Magnate Used Nightshade to Murder.*"

"You never told me the case you solved involved a media mogul!" I said to Violet as we walked down the street.

"You never asked," she replied with a small smile. "Besides, I do not think it is quite fair to call him a media mogul anymore, as the son of Edward Cornwall will not be in charge of anything apart from latrine duty at Pentonville Prison for the foreseeable future."

Violet, rather than picking the lock of the building in broad daylight, with dozens of people around, pressed the buzzer for apartment number 3, where Amelia had been found.

"Yes," answered a man's voice a moment later, and Violet raised her eyebrows at me.

"Hello, my name is Violet Despuis, I'm a detective investigating what happened to Amelia Waters. Would you mind letting me and my colleague up, please?"

"Of course," the man replied, and a moment later the door buzzed, indicating the lock was opened. We stepped into the building and made our way up a set of narrow, musty stairs. If I had asthma, I'd be reaching for my inhaler right about now.

"If she had a rich boyfriend, he certainly wasn't paying her rent," I panted as we made our way up the stairs. A single lightbulb hanging from the ceiling above lit the way; I felt like this was some kind of scene at the beginning of a horror movie, where they show the first two victims before something terrifying comes out and kills them.

Luckily, however, Violet and I made it all the way to the top floor without being eaten by aliens, and when she knocked on the solid, but ancient-looking wooden door, the man who answered almost immediately was definitely not rich.

Ok, so maybe I was jumping to conclusions. But the

man standing in front of us, looking to be in his early twenties, was wearing boxers and a ragged grey tank top. His black hair was messy, as he ran a hand through it, and he was squinting at us as if he'd just gotten up. "You're the investigators?" he asked, motioning for us to come in, which we did. The apartment was sparse to say the least. What furniture there was obviously came from Ikea, and the place looked like it hadn't seen a paintbrush or a contractor since the seventies, at least. This might have been one of the fancier neighborhoods in London, but this particular apartment wouldn't be getting any design awards anytime soon.

"Yes, Violet Despuis, and this is Cassie Coburn," Violet said. He held out a hand and we each shook it in turn.

"Jessie Hadid. Amelia's my roommate. You're that private detective that's in the news sometimes, right?"

"That is me, yes. I don't know if you've been told, Jessie, but Amelia died last night in the hospital."

"Damn," he said, running his hand through his hair again. "Poor girl. I liked Amelia. She was nice. Never really pictured her to be the type to do that sort of thing to herself, you know. I thought when I forgot my phone and I found her, that it may have been a stroke of luck. That maybe it would have been enough to save her."

"So, you were the one who found her?" Violet asked, and he nodded.

"Yeah. I'd gone out to the gym maybe fifteen

minutes earlier. I work out at Gymbox in Covent Garden, so it's only about a ten-minute walk from here. When I got there, I realized I'd forgotten my phone, and I hate working out without it so I jogged home to get it. When I got in I called out to her, but she didn't answer. Her shoes were still sitting by the front door, and I knew she was just planning on having a quiet afternoon in working on her maths stuff, so I thought it was weird. I went to knock on her door, but it wasn't latched, so it opened and I found her hanging there." Jessie Hadid shook his head. "It was the worst thing I've ever seen. I ran over to her and held her up for a minute, then ran to the kitchen and grabbed a knife and a chair and managed to cut her down. I called 999 and had them on speaker, the lady told me to try and find a pulse, and I did. They got here fast, and I hoped it was fast enough but I guess not."

"Do you always go to the gym at the same time?" Violet asked.

"Yeah, every day at two. Except Thursdays, I'm at college then. But why does that matter? She could have just waited until I'd gone to class."

"Amelia didn't kill herself; she was murdered," Violet replied, and I watched Jessie Hadid's face closely as the news sunk in. His eyes widened slightly, and he put his hand to his mouth before running it through his hair once more.

"No way. Seriously?"

"Yes," Violet nodded.

"Why aren't the coppers here, then?"

"Well, the police and I are currently having a disagreement about the cause of death. But do expect them to arrive eventually."

Jessie made his way to the small two-seater couch and sat down, staring at the floor. "Who would want to kill Amelia, though?"

"I was hoping you would be able to answer that question for us," Violet replied.

Jessie looked up at her and shrugged. "Honestly, I don't know. Amelia was a normal girl, really. She was super smart, one of those genius types, studying maths at Oxford."

"And she was staying in the city?" Violet asked, and Jessie grinned.

"I know, I thought the same thing. But she doesn't mind. Didn't mind. She grew up in the country, somewhere in darkest Nottinghamshire, so for her the city was big and exciting. I thought she was insane commuting to Oxford a few times a week, but she didn't seem to mind. Besides, she always told me the train she took to get up to Oxford was always empty, since she was always traveling the opposite way of most people. That was Amelia through and through, always looking for the good things in life."

"Do you know if she had a boyfriend?" I asked, and Jessie nodded.

"She did, yeah. They hadn't been together long

though; I haven't met him. She met him a few weeks ago, at her work."

"Where did she work?" I asked.

"British Horseracing Authority, she worked part-time at their head office in Holborn, doing administrative stuff. Mainly on weekends, when she didn't have classes on. She didn't work there much, but it gave her enough money to go out with her friends a few times a week."

"Who was her best friend?" Violet asked.

"Layla Chen, for sure. Another Oxford student. I'm not sure if she studies maths though. I didn't really see her much; as you can imagine this isn't exactly a prime setup for bringing home friends," Jessie said with a small smile.

"Do you mind if I look around Amelia's bedroom?" Violet asked, and Jessie indicated for her to go ahead. The two of us made our way into the spartan room; it was so small the double mattress took up the whole width of the room along the window. The plain white walls were left completely undecorated apart from a single postcard of Nottingham thumb tacked to the wall, featuring a building that looked a lot like the US Capitol building with a fountain in front of it and some pretty brick buildings on the left-hand side of the photo. Gothic red letters spelled out "Nottingham" in the middle of the postcard.

A small, plain white desk and chair took up the rest of the room; a laptop was on one side and several books about mathematical theory sat on the other. A cute Michael Kors purse sat against the side of the desk; like her clothes, Amelia had gone for a quality, mid-range designer brand for her choice of purse. Going by the amount of scuffing on the bottom, I would have guessed it was a couple years old. Amelia Waters had obviously been an extremely organized person. Going through her stuff revealed nothing much: there was some lint, an old receipt and a couple of tiny pebbles in one of her jacket pockets, and her purse had a few pens and notepads with some mathematical equations scribbled on them. An old iPhone in a Lifeproof case sat on top of the books; Violet immediately made her way to it and unlocked it in a matter of seconds, then tossed it to me.

"See if you can find the mystery boyfriend in there," she ordered as she looked through Amelia's purse, and I sat down on the bed and scrolled through Amelia's contacts list while Violet put on a pair of latex gloves before sitting down at the computer and opening it up. She made quick work of the password to gain access to the computer, as well.

"People, they are too predictable," Violet lamented as the computer's background came to life. "It would be a bigger challenge if they used passwords more difficult to guess than their birthdate."

I smiled to myself as I scrolled through the contacts. I found Layla Chen and jotted down her number on a post-it note I found in the desk drawer.

"*Ah, mais c'est interessant,*" Violet muttered to herself as she looked at the computer.

"What is it?" I asked.

"It appears as though someone has been here and deleted most of the data off this laptop," Violet said. She closed the lid and unplugged it, taking the cord and putting it in her purse. "Right. We are going, we need to find out what was on the laptop. Bring that phone with you as well."

"I have Layla Chen's phone number, we can organize a meet with her," I suggested.

"Good," Violet nodded. We made our way back into the main room where Jessie was waiting.

"If the police come by and look for Amelia's computer and phone, tell them that they are in my possession. They know how to find me."

"Sure. Hey, find who did this, will you? Amelia was too nice a person to have this happen to her. Whoever did it deserves to rot."

"Oh, do not worry. I will find Amelia's murderer. I am much smarter than nearly every criminal on this island."

"I thought you weren't supposed to promise results to friends and family," I said as we made our way down the stairs. "That's what every TV show about crime says."

"That only applies when there is a chance that the detective will not solve the case," Violet replied confidently. "Me, I can promise to find the murderer, and I do not have to worry about breaking my word."

I laughed as we continued back down towards the street. Violet was just so arrogantly confident sometimes it was unbelievable.

CHAPTER 5

$\mathcal{H}$alf an hour later Violet and I were sitting in the first-class carriage on the 10:43 from Paddington Station to Oxford, with Violet assuring me the trip would take just over an hour. She was leaning back in the seat with her eyes closed; I knew she was going through what facts we already knew in her head. Instead of bothering her, I turned my head out the window and admired the scenery as we left London; the skyscrapers soon turned into beautiful rolling fields, thatched-roof houses, and horses who didn't raise their heads from the grass on which they grazed as the train rolled past. It was postcard-quaint, and I made a mental note to come out this way sometime; after all, as amazing as London was, there was an incredible country here for me to explore as well.

When the train pulled into the station, Violet and I began the walk toward the city center.

"Layla Chen will meet with us when her classes finish for the day, at just after two this afternoon," Violet told me. "I thought that first, we should perhaps speak with her tutor at the college, and see what it was that Amelia was working on."

To be completely honest, I was only half listening to what Violet was telling me. We were just coming into Oxford center now, and my mouth dropped open as I saw the skyline. I thought the buildings at Stanford were impressive, but they had absolutely nothing on Oxford.

Tall, white-stone spires shot toward the sky, mingling with ancient-looking buildings. It was like walking into a cross between a medieval village and castle; it was as if the town and the university had both grown around each other and were now intertwined, like one couldn't live without the other.

"Amelia studied maths at Magdalen College," Violet told me. "Oxford, unlike other Universities, is split into a variety of different colleges. Each student attends a specific college. Amelia had the Magdalen College pin on her jacket hanging at the apartment."

"This place is amazing," I replied as we walked down High Street; everything about this place oozed class. Boutique hotels and modern cafés intermingled with *The* Oxford University Press Bookshop and art galleries. When we passed an ancient-looking stone building, with a thick wooden door topped with elaborate statues of horses surrounding blue-and-gold crests, I had to stop and admire the architecture. Steep gables on either side of the large tower that centered the building topped elaborate gothic windows and Juliette balconies; I stared in open wonder at the sophistication of the design which had to have been here for hundreds of years, at least.

"That is Brasenose College," Violet informed me as I stood there, mouth gaping open while a handful of students came out from the door, talking and laughing to each other, thick textbooks in hand. "And if this is the reaction you are going to have at every part of the college, please do let me know so that I can text Layla to push back our appointment."

"Sorry," I laughed. "I thought after having lived in London for so long that I'd be used to impressive buildings by now, but this place is something else."

"It certainly is," Violet agreed.

"How long has Oxford existed?" I asked.

"It is not known exactly when tutelage began here," Violet replied. "However, education has happened here since at least 1096. When Henry II banned English students from studying at the already-established *Université de Paris* in 1167, it grew significantly, and it was officially founded in 1248."

I let out a low whistle; it was almost inconceivable to me that students had walked these paths nearly a thousand years ago in the pursuit of knowledge, and were still doing so today. It was a completely humbling feeling.

A few minutes later we reached the walls of Magdalen College, which was pronounced "maudlin" for some reason. The main building was made of white and beige stone, in the same gothic style as the rest of the college. A large, square tower dominated the scene, rising high from the middle of the building, topped with pointed spires.

We entered through the main doors, made of grey wood with black iron bolts throughout, ducking under an ornate archway over which a statue of–I assumed– Mary Magdalene stood guard, surrounded by crests featuring a gothic letter 'M' and the college crest.

As we crossed into the grounds my mouth dropped open and I had to make an effort not to stop and gape once more. It was like we'd just walked into the main grounds of a castle–a castle with manicured lawns, a gorgeous leafy tree surrounded by perfectly main- tained ancient walls. It was no wonder so many of the world's greats came from here; the grounds of this college were nothing if not inspiring.

"Layla told me Amelia's tutor is a Professor Alan Knightly," Violet said as she expertly steered us into the building on our left, instantly transporting us into what I could only describe as Hogwarts, without the magic. Violet deftly managed the corridors and stair- cases as I followed in her footsteps, to the point where I began to suspect that this wasn't her first visit to this particular college. "While students here have tutors for individual classes, they also have one who oversees a student's entire studies over the course of their education here in Magdalen College."

We shortly found ourselves in the office of Professor Knightly, a tall man with a greying beard and a kind face who carried himself with confidence. He smiled at us when we came in, his eyes betraying his curiosity. I couldn't help but look at the office more than the man: The walls immediately behind us, lining either side of the door, made up a large bookcase, which was filled with volumes about maths. The professor sat in front of a large, old-style mahogany desk which sat on top of a deep red rug. Behind him, between two high windows which filled the room with warm light was a nice painting of some flowers on the water, and in the corner was a blackboard with figures on it, a piece of chalk sitting in a holder below.

Violet introduced us and he motioned for us to sit.

"I'm not sure what I can do for a detective," he said in a self-deprecating manner. "Unless you happen to have some trouble that requires expertise in maths."

"I'm afraid it is nothing so trivial," Violet replied. "One of your students was murdered yesterday."

"No! Murdered?" he exclaimed. "Oh, that's terrible news. Who was it?"

"Amelia Waters. I understand you were her tutor."

Professor Knightly nodded sadly. "Yes. Amelia is–

was—an extremely gifted scholar, and quite a nice human being. Have her parents been notified?"

"I am afraid I do not have that information. That is for the police," Violet replied.

"Of course, of course. I assume they will be by shortly as well. What can I do to help?"

"Tell me about Amelia's studies. What was she working on?"

Professor Knightly took his glasses off and pressed his fingers together in thought. "Amelia took part in her usual courses, which this semester were all mathematics-related. On top of that, however, along with a group of other students in the department, she was working on a mathematic algorithm. It was designed to determine algorithms to determine probability. Dear me. I imagine it won't ever be finished now."

"Why not?" I asked. "Aren't there other students in the group?"

Professor Knightly looked at me sadly. "Unfortunately, Jeremy Claridge was killed in a car accident back in March, and Amir Nader had a family emergency back in Egypt and had to fly home about two months ago. I believe his mother fell ill. And now this. I suppose Peter Alcott could continue with their project all on his own, but I wouldn't blame him if he wanted to abandon it."

"That does seem very unlucky," Violet said. "So this group had been working on this project for some time?"

Professor Knightly nodded. "Yes, they started on it at the beginning of the winter semester, so it's been about six months. I encouraged them; it was a challenging project but they worked well together. I was especially proud of them for continuing on after Jeremy's death. I'm afraid I don't know how close they were to completing it. I imagine after Amir left they must have taken a break from it."

My phone buzzed in my purse. Looking at the screen, I saw it was Jake calling, and I excused myself and made my way into the hallway.

"Hey," I answered.

"Hi, how are you feeling?" Jake asked. "I assume you've been discharged and are hunting down a murderer with Violet?"

"You know me too well," I laughed. "We're at Oxford right now. Amelia Waters was a student here, she was getting a degree in math."

"Well, I hope you find whoever did it. Unfortunately, on my front I have some bad news: I tried to get the body assigned to me, but since I left work as soon as Violet called me yesterday morning, I think my boss decided to take it out on me by saying no."

I sighed. "Well, that sucks. On the bright side, the other coroner will still call it a homicide, right? At Amelia's apartment Violet went through her computer, and she said someone had gone through it and deleted a bunch of stuff."

"Unfortunately, my esteemed colleague is rather old

school, and has a tendency to do whatever the police tell him to do. In this case, Detective Inspector Carlson made a visit to the morgue this morning, and after he left I went to speak to the doctor examining Amelia Waters' body. He's not going to label it as a murder."

"Even if it's obvious that's what it is?" I asked, incredulous.

I could almost feel Jake shrugging his shoulders on the other end of the line. "What can I say? Unfortunately, idiocy exists in all professions, even this one. I'm going to kindly suggest to my boss that he perhaps should review the cause of death finding on Waters' body, but I can't make any guarantees." Jake paused, then continued. "Anyway, can you text me when you and Violet come over here? I think I'm going to need forewarning on this one."

"Sure," I laughed. "Wait a minute! You're calling me instead of her because you don't want to have to be the one to tell her that her case isn't being declared a homicide."

"Sweetheart, I love to hear your voice at any time of the day, but yes, that's at least 80 percent of the reason I called you with this info and not her."

"You're impossible!" I replied, laughing.

"Well you're really going to hate this then, but I have to call off our date for tonight if that's ok. I'm going to have to work some overtime tonight."

"That's all right," I replied. "I'm not entirely sure my mind would be in a date anyway, right now."

"All right, I'll talk to you soon. Don't get into too much trouble. After all, you did almost die twenty-four hours ago."

"With Violet, that's pretty much a guarantee."

"Well, if you get arrested let me know and I'll come bail you out."

"That's the sweetest thing you've ever said to me," I teased. "Talk to you soon."

I hung up the phone just as Violet walked out of the office. "Professor Knightly did not have much more to offer us. I assume that was Jake?"

I nodded. "You're not going to like what he has to say."

CHAPTER 6

Unfortunately for Violet, we couldn't go back to London to yell at one of the pathologists at the morgue until after we met with Layla Chen. As we still had a couple of hours before we had to meet with her, Violet and I decided to grab a quick lunch. It seemed Violet's knowledge of where to eat wasn't limited to London alone; she immediately led me toward a cute café in a red-brick building with a wooden sign above white square windows announcing "Organic Deli Café."

While I was initially apprehensive–this seemed like the sort of place that made their chips with kale instead of potatoes–I was pleasantly surprised to find a full menu board, and eagerly ordered a sourdough BLT. Violet ordered a tofu scramble, which I did my best not to scrunch my nose at. We sat at a cute round table and discussed the case.

"I do not like that three of the students in that group are now gone. I believe we should find Peter Alcott–after all, he is the only one of the four students working on that project who is still in the area."

"You think we should warn him to take a holiday far away from here for a while, or something?" I asked.

"That, but also we should investigate him as a suspect."

"True," I conceded. After all, maybe he was knocking off his group mates for fun. "Though maybe it is just a coincidence. Maybe Jeremy Claridge did just die in a car crash, and Amir Nader really did go back to Egypt."

"Perhaps," Violet said. "We need to investigate further. If we are lucky Layla Chen will be able to enlighten us. We also need to look at the alibi of the Professor Knightly, he says he was at the school teaching when Amelia Waters was murdered."

"You don't seriously think a professor here could have done it!" I exclaimed.

Violet turned to me with a smile. "You would be surprised at the number of respectable people I have had arrested in the past. Heads of state, business leaders, doctors, professors–the allure of crime does not avoid certain careers completely. I had to ask. After all, the professor is the unique link between the four students, as far as we are aware."

"Fair enough," I replied. "I think you're right though. Three of the four people in the group disappearing in one way or another is a pretty big coincidence. So we talk to Layla Chen, what then?"

"Well, hopefully she will be able to tell us about Amelia's romantic life. It is always good to keep all avenues of investigation open, as we may be incorrect about the maths students being killed or disappearing being linked to Amelia's death. I would also like to know more about this algorithm the students were working on. We will have to find Peter Alcott. Professor Knightly was able to give me his mobile number. And of course, there is a certain medical examiner who needs a lesson in basic anatomy back in London. I hope you did not have any plans for the rest of the day, Cassie. Murder investigation tends to be rather intensive."

I leaned back in my chair. "As long as you promise not to poison me again."

"I also cured you," Violet protested. "I believe you are undervaluing my contribution to science and to your former chosen profession, for which I am well aware you still have a significant passion. After all, my discovery did save your life."

"Which wouldn't have needed saving in the first place if you hadn't left freshly baked poisoned brownies out on the table," I pointed out.

"All the same, I am happy that my antidote worked, and that you are not dead."

"So am I," I replied, smiling at Violet. I meant it, and I still didn't take that feeling for granted. After all, for a long time after my accident, I found myself wondering what the point of living at all was. And now, here in London, I was finally discovering that there was life after losing 5 percent use in my hand, that it was possible for me to have a life outside of the medical field and still be happy.

I had applied for medical school here, although I still wasn't sure if I was going to register if I was accepted. Right now, it was just a potential plan. But it was a plan that had me thinking about the future, which was a good thing.

I picked up my sandwich and bit into it. "Just think, if it wasn't for your antidote I wouldn't get to eat the best sourdough sandwich I've had in weeks."

"Perhaps if your life did not seemingly revolve entirely around food–and mainly junk food, to make it worse–then you would not have found yourself in that situation in the first place."

"Enjoying the finer things in life is one of the pleasures of living, and quinoa does not qualify as a 'finer thing,'" I replied with my mouth full, and Violet rolled her eyes before pulling out her phone and beginning to type.

"Trying to find Peter Alcott?"

"Exactly," Violet nodded. "If what we suspect is correct, he is either a murderer, or his life is in danger. Either way, we must get into contact with him."

Checking my phone, I noticed it was time for us to go and meet with Layla Chen, so I scarfed down the last bite of my sandwich and we made our way to the door.

We met Layla Chen at what Violet informed me was known as the New Building Lawns. She was tall, with shoulder-length black hair and almond-shaped eyes. Her bag was slung casually over her shoulder, her smile came fairly easily despite the circumstances, and I had a sense that she was normally a very outgoing and friendly person. The lawns were gorgeously manicured, with a few stone paths running between the lawns. In the far corner, on the opposite side of the lawns from the New Building, was a huge tree whose leaves blew gently in the early autumn breeze. The three of us sat down on a bench by the corner of the new building and Violet began to ask Layla, whose eyes were red from tears, about her murdered friend.

"Is there anyone you can think of who would have wanted to hurt Amelia?" Violet asked, and Layla shook her head.

"God, no. If you'd met Amelia, you'd know she was the type of person who could befriend anyone. I always told her she should be a judge or something, because criminals would thank her for sentencing them to jail. That was the kind of effect she had on people."

"So, there were no disagreements with anyone lately?"

"Well, she was going to move out of her flat with Jessie when the lease came up in December. She decided that after a year of living in London she wanted to be closer to Oxford. Amelia liked to think she was the partying city-girl type, but she really wasn't."

"She was more the type to stay in and read her books?"

"Yeah, definitely." Layla laughed, which mingled in with a sob at one point. "Although I'll never forget the first time she tried Indian food. You know, she had never had anything other than English fare and the occasional Chinese meal down in Nottingham? The first time she ate butter chicken it was like her whole life had changed completely. I remember, we'd had a few drinks first, and she asked the waiter if there were any flats for let nearby so she could live close enough to the restaurant to eat there three times a day." Amelia giggled, which quickly caused a few errant tears to fall from her eyes, which she quickly wiped away. Violet gave her a moment to collect herself before continuing.

"Was Jessie upset about the fact she was leaving?"

Amelia shrugged. "Not especially. It's London, finding a new flatmate isn't exactly difficult these days."

"And it wasn't like he wanted to be more than roommates and she didn't?" I asked, and Layla gave me a small smile.

"No, there was absolutely no chance of that. Jessie's gay."

Well, there went the jealous roommate theory.

"What do you know about the project Amelia was

working on with the other people in her group?" Violet asked.

"Not a huge amount, really. I'm studying chemistry, not maths, so we didn't really chat that much about our classes. I do know it was an algorithm they were working on; it was designed to take multiple pieces of data and figure out the original equation that would give out all those figures."

"Really? You are certain that is what they were working on?"

"Well, I'm pretty sure. That was how Amelia described it. I'm really not that good at maths though, so I could have got it wrong." Layla shrugged.

"And what about her boyfriend? Jessie said she was seeing someone?"

Layla smiled. "She was. They'd only been seeing each other for about a week, maybe two. I had a bad feeling about him though."

"Why do you say that?"

"Well for one thing, he gave her a pair of beautiful sapphire earrings on their first date. What kind of guy does that? Amelia said he made her feel like a princess, but I think that was what he liked about her. After all, Amelia was still very much a country girl; any man who spoke to her for more than thirty seconds could figure that out. I'm pretty sure he was going to take advantage of her, keeping her hooked by buying her pretty things. I definitely don't begrudge her having her fun, so I pretended to be supportive, but I knew it was never going to be a long-term sort of thing."

"Do you know his name?"

"Only a first name: Oliver. He was into horse racing though, since they met at her work, and she mentioned once that he planned on taking her to the Champion Stakes later this month. I never met him, but she showed me a picture of the two of them together."

"Oliver. And you say he was rich?"

"Oh, definitely. It wasn't just the earrings, he bought her a Balenciaga handbag as well. Do you know how much those cost? It was adorable seeing how happy Amelia was with the bag–I mean, I would be too if I had a handbag worth fifteen hundred pounds, but I don't think Amelia quite understood what was expected of her in exchange for those sorts of gifts."

"You mean that Oliver gave her that stuff so she'd sleep with him," I replied, as Violet was busy typing away on her phone. Layla gave me a knowing smile.

"Exactly. Amelia was pretty naïve when it came to men. Although I don't think their relationship got quite that far. You know, I've spent the last fortnight wishing their relationship would end quickly, for Amelia's sake." Tears welled up in Layla's eyes and she brushed them away. "Now, now I wish…"

Her voice trailed off as her eyes grew distant, the grief overtaking her for a moment.

"Layla," Violet said softly, holding up her phone. "Is this Oliver, the man Amelia was dating?"

"Yes," she replied. "That's definitely him."

I took the phone from Violet and had a look at the image she had opened. Smiling at me was a thin man who looked to be in his late thirties, with brown hair that was just starting to grey around the edges. He was holding a glass of champagne and laughing in the photo; I could see just from this still that he was charismatic.

"Thank you, Layla," Violet said. "And I am sorry about your friend. I will do my best to find whoever killed her."

"Thank you," Layla replied. "Amelia was a precious human being. She didn't deserve to die. I don't care what the police think, she never would have killed herself. Thanks for believing that."

Layla got up and walked off; I noticed her wiping away at her eyes once more. It had to be a difficult day for her, for sure.

"Well, that was an illuminating conversation. Now, we go back to London."

"Are we going to the morgue?"

"No. A man who is an idiot today will almost certainly still be an idiot tomorrow. I can yell at that *imbécile* of a pathologist any time. Right now, finding the murderer who may have Peter Alcott in his sights–and who may have already struck given the lack of a response to my texts–is the bigger priority."

CHAPTER 7

*N*inety minutes later we were back in London. Violet spent almost the entire train ride texting, and when we arrived back at Paddington Station we walked the couple of meters to Paddington Green Police Station.

DCI Williams was sitting at his desk on the third floor–the second in UK terms, a mix-up that led to me meeting Violet in the first place—the brow under his short red hair furrowed in concentration; he didn't notice us until Violet and I each sat down in the visitors' chairs across from him.

"Violet!" he said as he looked up. "You're just the woman I want to see! Don't tell me you've added mind reading to your list of abilities."

"My powers remain firmly in the realm of what is realistically possible," Violet replied. "I am after information on a fatal accident that occurred on the A40 in

March." Now I knew what Violet had been doing on her phone on the train ride home.

DCI Williams sighed as he leaned back in his chair. "Is that your way of telling me you're not here to work on my diamond theft case?"

"Is that the "Terrible Trio" thing I saw as the headline on The London Post-Tribune this morning?" I asked.

"Yes, that's them. This is the third robbery they've pulled off in as many months, and as much as we keep denying this to the press, we have nothing."

"As precious as the diamonds that were stolen may have been, they are nothing compared to a human life, which is the theft we are currently attempting to prevent."

"You're looking for data for someone who's dead though?"

"Yes, and if I am correct, someone killed that person, and has killed two others as well."

"Recently?"

"Yesterday."

"I haven't heard of any new murders in London."

"That is because the pack of *imbéciles* who make up a large portion of the Metropolitan Police force as well as the staff at the Westminster Public Mortuary are happier to chalk obvious murders up as a suicide so that they are able to eat their lunch sooner."

"Which particular imbecile are you referring to this time?" DCI Williams asked, leaning back in his chair.

"Detective Inspector Carlson," Violet replied, and I saw the corners of DCI Williams' lips twitch with a smile.

"Oh, he must have loved you," he replied. "Even I will admit that my esteemed colleague is perhaps one sandwich short of a picnic."

"Well that is a nicer way of putting it than I would have done," Violet replied. "Now, can you get me the file?"

"I suppose so. Let me go down to the storage room and find what I have."

DCI Williams got up and made his way toward the lifts. As he entered, Violet grabbed the file already on his desk and pulled it toward us.

"If you actually manage to solve the big jewellery heist before DCI Williams gets back here, I will only eat smoothie bowls and quinoa salads for a week," I teased, and Violet grinned at me.

"I suspect that even I will not be able to solve the case so quickly. However, it is interesting all the same. Perhaps when we have solved this case I will turn my attentions to this one."

"I'll make sure to clear my calendar," I joked.

"It is interesting, though," Violet noted. "Not interesting enough to stop investigating a murder, mind you, but interesting all the same. Three men, it took them four minutes to get in and out of a diamond store on Oxford Street, and the police have no leads. That, however, is not saying very much."

I looked through the pictures when Violet was finished with them, but had to admit, I didn't blame the police at all. It just looked like a pilfered safe, and three masked men on the CCTV footage. Not exactly a lot to go by.

About five minutes later DCI Williams returned, holding a folder in his hands and looking a little bit more annoyed than he had when he went down. I couldn't help but notice the right shoulder of his suit now had a significant amount of dust on it.

"Please make this worth it for me," he said, flopping back down into his chair. "I had four evidence boxes fall on me. Thank goodness they were all sealed."

"You should take the stairs rather than the lift," Violet replied, never taking her eyes off the file she'd blatantly taken off DCI Williams' desk. "It is healthier."

"Thanks for the tip. Now, what do you have?"

Violet handed the file back to DCI Williams and leaned back in her chair, closing her eyes. "You are looking for three men. One is one hundred and eighty-three centimeters tall, the second is one hundred and eighty-five, and the third only one hundred and seventy-seven, possibly one hundred and seventy-eight. The first man is the ringleader. Going by the contents that they stole they knew exactly what was worth the most money. They immediately stole the diamonds, and a few watches and left the other precious stones. In fact it is rather strange how much they left. There is not much else to be told from the photos."

"Is that it?" DCI Williams said, and I could tell he was slightly disappointed. Violet shrugged.

"You give me three grainy, still photographs of men in masks. Even I am not a miracle worker."

"I have video footage as well, of both the interior during the robbery and of the outside of the building."

"Email it to me, I will look at it when I have a chance," Violet said. "Now, I need my file. I have an actual murder to solve."

DCI Williams passed it over to her, and Violet stood up. "Is there a room where we can look at this?"

"At least one of the interview rooms should be empty," DCI Williams said. "Thanks for the tips about their heights."

Violet and I got up and made our way into one of the interview rooms, a boring grey rectangle with a table and three chairs that were bolted to the floor. It wasn't exactly Oxford, but it would have to do.

I sat down across from Violet as she opened the file. She passed the photos of the scene over to me as she scanned the written reports.

The first picture was of some skid marks, leading to a wrecked motorcycle on the side of the road. There were some other pictures of the motorcycle, which had suffered extensive damage to the right-hand side on which it lay. Finally, a photo showed Jeremy Claridge being attended to by EMTs. He had been wearing a helmet, and other protective gear. It just hadn't been enough.

After a couple of minutes Violet and I swapped information, and I read through the file on the accident.

He had crashed less than a thousand feet from where we were, on the A40. The report suggested he lost control, there was no evidence any other vehicle was involved. The accident occurred just after three in the morning, and there were no witnesses. It had been a clear night, with no rain in the previous twenty-four hours, and Jeremy Claridge had no drugs or alcohol in his system when he died. One resident living nearby said she thought she heard tires squealing just after the crash, but since there was no corroboration, and even she admitted she may have still been confused as she was half asleep, nothing came of it.

"Let me guess, you have tons of proof that this was actually done on purpose," I said to Violet, who shook her head.

"Sadly, no. I cannot say for certain. However, there are certain indications that it was not an accident. The woman's account, saying she heard squealing tires *after* the crash, for example. And the odds of a man who was stone-cold sober completely losing control of his motorcycle on a straight, double-lane road with no traffic are fairly low. There is also a little bit of white paint on the rear of the motorcycle. However, I do not know if it was from the accident, or from a previous minor incident."

"I'm with you. I think we should assume he was run off the road."

"I do not like assumptions, but we will stick with that as being the most likely scenario for now. I will endeavour to find out whether Amir Nader is really in Egypt or not, as well."

We packed up the file and made our way back to DCI Williams, who was still poring over his case.

"Thank you for this," Violet said.

"So, was that guy murdered too?"

"We cannot know for certain, but it appears to be likely, especially given the disappearance of another student at Oxford, and the murder of a third."

"Well, as much as I'd like to help you on that, I can't trample over a colleague and force him to treat a case as a murder. Besides, as you can see, I'm busy with my own investigation. Apparently, the higher-ups are giving me an entire task force to help solve this case."

"At least now you can search the databases for their heights, that sounds like a boring job for the least experienced officer on your task force."

"Right. Thanks for the help with that. I'll email you the videos, if you can look at them when you get a chance."

"I will, although I do not guarantee that it will be before we solve this case. Also, I need you to look for someone for me."

"Yes?"

"A Peter Alcott. Student at Oxford. This is his mobile number," she said, scribbling on a piece of paper. "He has not replied to my texts, and I fear that he is either my murderer, or my murderer's next victim. If the latter, I would prefer it if he remained alive, as he may be quite useful to me."

"What do you want me to do if we find him alive and well?"

"Send him to me. We need to have a chat. And keep a car outside of his home for the night. If he is to be the next victim, I do not know how long it will take before they strike again."

"Will do. You're sure this is a murder then?"

"There is absolutely no doubt about it. And if I hadn't accidentally poisoned Cassie and the victim had not ended up in the bed next to her at the Royal London, whoever did it would have got away with it, too," Violet said as we got up to leave.

"Wait… what?" a confused DCI Williams said as Violet walked off.

"Don't ask," I said. "Thanks for the help." I left a confused-looking DCI Williams at his desk as the two of us left the police station.

CHAPTER 8

*D*eciding there was nothing left for us to do that day, Violet decided to go home and think about the case, while I went home and took Biscuit, my cute little orange cat, for a walk on his leash. I ran through the case in my head, trying to re-organize the facts, but I couldn't think of anything that might help.

I figured maybe if I found out something about Amelia Waters' life, maybe a detail that would end up being important, that could be useful, but scouring her social media turned out to be basically useless; she wasn't much of a user of Facebook or Instagram, and what accounts she did have had their privacy settings turned onto high.

Eventually I walked down to Gloucester Road to get a B-Rex burger and sweet potato fries from Byron, which was one of my favorite nearby places to get a quick burger fix. I took my burger home and settled in to watch some Netflix with Biscuit for the rest of the night, the whole time my mind wandering as I wondered who would have killed Amelia Waters.

I woke up the next morning to find I'd gotten a text from Violet—at two thirty-six in the morning, of course—to come over before eight. I groaned as I looked at the clock and saw that was ten minutes away. Apparently Violet didn't know the meaning of sleeping in.

I rolled out of bed, Biscuit meowing at me in protest.

"I know, I don't want to leave the nice warm bed either," I told him, patting him on the head. I left him out some food and grabbed a banana from the fridge—I wasn't about to trust any food Violet was going to offer—before running a brush through my hair quickly and throwing on some jeans and a t-shirt, topping them with a cardigan. As I ran out the door I checked my watch again, it was only 8:03. I'd made pretty good time.

The weather today was a lot worse than the day before. The grey clouds overhead threatened to open and drench London with rain, and I grabbed my small umbrella that always sat by the door as I left, hugging my cardigan closer to me as a cool breeze passed through the street.

The stiff breeze had caused my landlady Mrs. Michaels' newspaper to blow away from her door and down the steps, and I almost tripped over it on my way up them.

I grabbed the paper and made my way up the couple of steps to her front door, intending to drop it off once more–and probably secure it just a little bit better–when the picture on the front page caught my eye.

It was a picture of me!

More specifically, it was a picture of Violet and me. I stopped in my tracks and opened the front of the paper to look at the headline.

Despuis Ignores Police, Investigates Suicide

It was *The London Post-Tribune*, I noticed, the same paper whose heir apparent Violet had just nailed for murder thanks to my eating those brownies. I didn't know the details of the case, but I knew that much, and as I read the article my heart sank. It was a total hatchet job.

French Private Investigator Violet Despuis has found herself in hot water with the law, as she has refused to accept the police's finding that an Oxford student living in London had committed suicide, and has been interrogating the woman's grieving friends and acquaintances despite explicit orders from the London Metropolitan Police to stay away from the case.

"While it is true that in the past Miss Despuis' work has led to the arrest of a few criminals, she is blatantly flouting a direct order and harassing grieving acquaintances of a woman who it has been determined not only by us, but also

by a pathologist, committed suicide," a source inside the Metropolitan Police force told The London Post-Tribune *last night.*

While Miss Despuis has made something of a name for herself, the police consider her latest actions to be harassment, and it is obvious that by interrogating grief-stricken acquaintances of a suicidal young woman, she has crossed a line of decency and needs to be stopped.

I dropped the paper on the ground in disgust; if it had belonged to me I probably would have torn it into pieces. How dare they imply that Violet was wrong, that she was *interrogating* family members? She could be cold and calculating quite a lot of the time, but Violet was also a good actress, and tended to be warm and polite to people when they answered her questions so soon after a loved one's death.

My jaw still tight with anger, I half-jogged up to Violet's house, a few houses down the street from my basement suite, and made my way up the steps, without even noticing the man coming toward me until I'd ran straight into him.

"Sorry! Sorry," he said, reaching out to steady me. "I'm so sorry!"

"It's all right," I replied with a laugh. "I'm sorry too, I definitely wasn't watching where I was going."

"Neither was I, I was looking for an address on this street, number eighteen."

"Oh, you're here to see Violet," I exclaimed, giving the man a better look. He was tall and lanky, at least six

foot three, with thin brown hair plastered to his fore-
head and nervous-looking brown eyes that kept
darting around here and there. He was dressed casually
but nicely, wearing jeans and a polo shirt, carrying a
messenger bag.

"I am, you know her then?"

"Yeah, I'm heading over there now," I said,
motioning for him to follow me up the steps to her
place. I knocked on the front door and a moment later
Violet answered, wearing skinny jeans under a light
red oversized top. She was on the phone.

Violet opened the door wide and the two of us
entered. She motioned for the man to sit in one of the
chairs in the study, which he did. I sat on the long
couch next to Violet. "*Nem 'afahum. Shukraan,*" she said
into the phone before hanging up.

"Hey, Violet. You have a guest."

She looked over at the man and nodded. "Peter
Alcott, I presume?"

He nodded. "Yes." He kept looking around, like
something was going to jump out from behind the
couch and bite his head off, or something.

"Have the police been in contact with you?" she
asked, and he shook his head.

"No. Well, I went and saw them, but not since. I
haven't been home since yesterday morning, when I
heard what happened to Amelia." His voice wavered a
few times, Peter Alcott was obviously nervous and on
the verge of tears.

"How did you find out what happened?"

"I have a friend in one of Layla Chen's classes. He told me. As soon as he told me she was dead, I knew. I knew it wasn't a coincidence. They were coming for us."

"Who?" Violet asked, leaning forward on the couch. "Who is doing this to your group?"

"I don't know!" Peter practically wailed. "I wish I knew. Then at least I'd know who to look for. But they're all gone! It can't be a coincidence."

"It is not a coincidence. They were all murdered."

"I know," he replied. "But no one believes me. When Jeremy died, I was a bit suspicious. After all, the guy knew his way around a motorcycle. He'd been riding them on his parents' farm since he was just a wee lad. For him to crash on the road like that, it seemed unlikely, but accidents do happen, right? Then when Amir just up and left for Egypt, without saying a thing to any of us? That was even more strange. The guy was about as outgoing as you could get. He would have never left without saying goodbye. He was the type who would have asked us what souvenirs we wanted him to bring back. He'd never mentioned his mum being sick, and he spoke about his family back there all the time. No, I really didn't like the fact that he left like that. And now Amelia. Someone's coming for all of us, and they're making it look like an accident."

"Yes," Violet replied. "Is that why you did not answer my text messages yesterday?"

"Exactly," Peter nodded. "I thought you were one of them. I thought you were going to come to get me, too. So I ignored you, and I went to the police. I went and saw the man who was investigating Amelia's death, since I didn't know who else to go to, and he just laughed at me and told me she killed herself. As I was leaving, he muttered to himself about how Violet Despuis was meddling in his case, making other people think Amelia was killed instead of accepting the suicide. Then I knew your text was real, but I'd already thrown away my phone and couldn't reply. So I looked you up, found out where you live, and came here."

"You did the right thing, Peter," Violet said. "It is true, I believe that you are in all likelihood in mortal danger."

"Why, though? Why are they killing us?"

"I suspect it is because of the project you are working on."

"The algorithm? The one that finds the equation used to generate multiple integers? But why would anyone want that?"

Violet shrugged. "I do not know yet. I have Amelia's laptop, it appears that someone deleted a large number of the files from her computer, including anything to do with the algorithm. Unfortunately, I was unable to recover it. Do you have a copy?"

Peter reached down into his messenger bag and pulled out a MacBook. "Yes, yes, of course. I brought it here. We finished it up a couple of weeks ago, Amelia and me. You're saying someone's going to kill me because of an algorithm a group of us made for college?"

"I believe that is the reason, yes." Violet got up and motioned for Peter to put his computer on the nearby desk. He did so and sat on the chair while Violet and I stood on either side of it.

"How does it work, your algorithm?"

"Well, it's pretty simple, really," Peter answered. "You input a bunch of figures, whatever figures you have. Obviously the more that are available, the better. Then, you run the algorithm, and it will give you a whole list of equations that can result in those figures being the result."

"Ah, I think I understand," Violet said as Peter opened the program. It was a simple black screen with a white flashing bar indicating where to type.

"Just enter in a series of numbers, separated by commas," Peter instructed, and Violet typed away for a minute: *-1,1,3,5,7,9,11,13,15,17,19*

When she pressed enter, two equations showed up below:

$2x-3$

$x+2$

She smiled. "I like it."

"It's kind of cool, isn't it?" Peter asked, his fear momentarily forgotten as he showed off his brain-child.

"Are you doing it for a specific class?"

"No," Peter replied. "Professor Knightly knew about it, of course, and so did a number of our other professors. And a good chunk of students as well. It started off as an assignment for a class, and we submitted a very rudimentary model of it as our assignment. But when the class finished, the four of us decided to continue working on it. After all, we saw the potential that kind of algorithm had, and it was a great way to challenge ourselves. You're really saying this is the reason someone is killing the people in our group?"

The fear in Peter's eyes had returned, his momentary respite from the reality of the situation facing him finished.

Violet nodded. "How are you, financially?"

"I'm pretty well-off, luckily. My parents both work as executives in the city."

"I recommend that you go overseas. Today. Do not wait, do not go home. I want you to take a cab from here directly to Heathrow. You are to contact nobody–and I mean nobody–that you have previously known until I have found the murderer. When you are settled, create yourself a new email account under a pseudonym and email this address," Violet said, handing him a card. As Peter took it, I noticed his hand trembling slightly.

"Where should I go?" he asked.

"Anywhere that is not England," Violet replied.

"I've always wanted to see the Balkans," Peter said so quietly it was almost to himself. I felt sorry for him;

he had just figured out that he was the target of a murderer, and was now being told that he had to leave his entire life behind for the foreseeable future.

"Can I have a copy of the algorithm?" Violet asked.

"Sure, yeah," Peter said glumly, accepting the USB key Violet handed him and plugging it into his computer. He copied the program onto the key and handed it back to Violet. "There you go. Hopefully that doesn't mean people are going to start coming after you, too."

"It would not be the first time. I am better prepared to handle that sort of situation than you. And you say you cannot think of anyone who would want to kill for the software, or any reason why you would be killed for it?"

"No. No, of course not. It's just a stupid university project. It's an exercise for the brain only. What kind of use could anyone ever have for it?"

"That is the question that we need to answer," Violet said thoughtfully. She went over to her computer and typed away for a few minutes. When she was done, she handed a piece of paper to Peter. "You are booked on British Airways, you leave Gatwick at 12:25 this afternoon for Venice. From there, rent a car and drive to the Balkans. Enjoy your holiday. I am certain that when you return, the administration at Oxford will understand your absence. Do not forget to email me, but not from your regular address."

"Thanks," Peter said to Violet quietly. For such a tall man, he was extremely quiet. "I appreciate it."

"Thank me by going to the airport and not getting yourself killed," Violet replied, and I had to hide a smile. That was about as sentimental as Violet got.

"Ok. Ok, I'll go right now," he said. "Thanks again."

Peter left, and Violet sighed as she closed the door. "When you came in, I was on the phone."

"I might not have your powers of observation, but even I picked up on that. You were speaking in Arabic?"

"Yes, you have the good ear," Violet said, nodding appreciatively. "I was on the phone with some people I know in the government in Egypt. They have no record of Amir Nader entering Egypt in the previous twelve months. And before that I was on the phone with a woman I know who works at UK Border Control, and she tells me that they have no record that Amir Nader has left England except for two years ago, for two weeks."

"So, his body's lying in a ditch somewhere waiting to be discovered."

"In all likelihood, yes."

I shook my head. "That's crazy. All these murders were made to look like something else. A motorcycle crash, someone visiting a sick relative overseas, and a suicide."

"Someone really wants that algorithm. And now that they managed to access Amelia Waters' computer, they have it. I hope whoever did it does not want Peter Alcott dead that badly."

"So, you don't think he's a suspect anymore then?"

Violet shrugged. "Who knows. He was convincing, but I have met many murderers in the past who were just as convincing."

"Wait, so you possibly just told a murderer to flee the country?"

"I would rather allow a murderer to flee than to allow an innocent man to be killed by remaining here," Violet replied. "Besides, it is not as though the world is infinitely vast; if it turns out he is the murderer and he has fled, I will find him all the same."

I smiled at Violet's arrogance. "So, what's the plan for today? We need to find out why anyone would want that algorithm?"

"Yes, we do," Violet said thoughtfully. "That is an interesting question, that. Still, I want to talk with Oliver Hollingsworth, Earl of Norwich."

"Wait, the guy she was dating was an Earl? That's like, important here, right?"

Violet tried to hide a smile. "Yes, the peerage in Great Britain is still significant. Oliver Hollingsworth is a man of both great riches—he is known to be one of the savviest investors in the country—and of great power. The earrings and handbag that Amelia was given were proof the owner was a man of means, and when Layla told me his name was Oliver, I immediately thought of Hollingsworth, a man who keeps a large stable in Norwich which has produced a large number of the UK's most famous horses over the past fifteen years."

"Oh yeah, those sound like normal facts any normal person should know," I said. How on earth did Violet know *that* off the top of her head?

"It is my job to know these things; if I did not know them we would still not know who Amelia Waters' boyfriend was."

"True, so what's the plan?"

"We go to find him at his club," Violet replied with a smile. "But first, we are going to have to change."

CHAPTER 9

*S*o far in my life, when someone asked me if I wanted to go to a club, they meant pounding music, questionable dancing and copious amounts of alcohol.

It was absolutely nothing like this.

We were at the corner of Pall Mall and Waterloo Square, staring at a phenomenal white building. Stand-alone both in location and in style, the Athenaeum Club was unlike anything I'd ever seen before. The three-story tall white building was style and class epitomized. The entrance was marked by six Corinthian columns, topped with a golden statue of Athena herself, which shone brightly even on this overcast day. The exterior wall of the second floor was decorated with a bas-relief frieze against a blue background, and the third floor was set back slightly, allowing for a large balcony space.

No wonder Violet had made us change.

She was now wearing a form-fitting grey dress that went down to just past her knees, with a gold belt to hold it in place. I had borrowed from Violet's closet and was now wearing an azure dress with a Queen Anne neckline that just reached my knees. My normal purse was now a black designer clutch, and I'd traded in my sneakers for a pair of kitten heels–with my knee never having gone quite back to 100 percent, high heels had a tendency to irritate it after long periods of time.

We entered through the wooden doors, and made our way toward a well-dressed man.

"We are guests of Sir Charles Dartmouth," Violet told him. "He is expecting us in the coffee room."

"Of course," the man replied deferentially, bowing slightly to us. "Please, follow me."

We were led through to a room so incredible I felt small and insignificant just standing in it. Thick, deep red curtains with gold accents hung from the windows, while old-world style chandeliers hung low from the ornate ceilings. The plush carpet was the same deep red as the curtains, also accented with gold. The white walls were tastefully decorated, with just a hint of gold here and there, and the room was filled with small square tables that allowed four people to sit at each.

A low hum from the club members floated across the room while waiters danced between the tables carrying trays of food and drink; I was pretty sure just one piece of cutlery here was worth more than all the dishes I owned combined. This was obviously a meeting place of the elite, and I tried not to look around and gape as I followed Violet between the rows of mahogany tables.

As soon as he saw us, a tall, thin man in a tweed jacket with a small grey mustache and thinning hair stood up with a smile.

"Violet Despuis!" he said, opening his arms wide as Violet made her way toward him and double kissed him on the cheek.

"Charles," she replied with a smile.

"You look as ravishing as ever, Violet," he said. "And your friend as well."

"This is Cassie Coburn," Violet said as I held out a hand, which the man promptly shook. "Cassie, this is Sir Charles Dartmouth, an old friend."

"You must be quite the woman, to manage to be friends with Violet," he told me with a warm smile that reached his eyes. His accent was the epitome of high English; he sounded like he could have been best friends with Prince Charles. In fact, given the clientele that seemed to be here, I wouldn't have been surprised if he was.

"Thanks," I said, blushing. "She can be a handful, but she is very interesting."

"Oh yes," Charles said. "When I got a phone call from her last night requesting an invitation to break-fast here at The Athenaeum, how could I say no? After all, Violet does not make social calls, and so whatever she has planned is bound to be entertaining."

Violet couldn't hide her small smile. "Perhaps."

Just then a waiter came by, handing us each a menu, and Violet ordered a coffee while Charles and I each ordered some tea.

"So how do you know Violet?" I inquired politely, and Charles smiled.

"We have similar business interests," he replied.

"Charles deals in information," Violet clarified. "Well, that and the stock market."

"Information is far more valuable than technology ever will be," Charles told me. "But it does help to have a more legitimate front. Now tell me, because I am curious, what is it about you that Violet makes you the only human being she has ever taken along with her on a case?"

"So, you saw the picture of us in *The London Post-Tribune* this morning?" I asked, and got a wink in reply. "Well, I think the main thing I have going for me is that I don't complain too much when Violet poisons me with nightshade by accident and I end up in the hospital."

"You have done nothing *but* complain about that since yesterday!" Violet replied, while Charles burst out laughing.

"Stories like that are why I adore Violet's company," Charles said. "Although I must say, I would absolutely not have the fortitude to handle those sorts of adventures on a daily basis, I prefer to hear about them later in a comfortable setting such as this one."

The waiter returned with our drinks just then, and while Charles and I placed breakfast orders–I imagined if anywhere was going to make a delicious eggs benedict it was here–but Violet declined. I wondered why, but I was sure Violet had a plan. When the waiter left, she turned toward me.

"Charles here has placed himself perfectly to get a good view of the show. If you look directly behind me, the man at the next table facing us, you should recognize him as Oliver Hollingsworth, the man who was dating Amelia Waters at the time of her death."

I looked behind Violet and sure enough, the same older man with the charming smile was currently entertaining three other men, the quartet all dressed in full three-piece suits.

"Now, if you will excuse me," Violet continued, "I need to eliminate a suspect from our inquiries."

Violet got up from the table and I watched with bated breath as she made her way toward the table next to ours. I had no idea what was about to happen.

"Oliver Hollingsworth, I thought you would be here," Violet said, making her way to their table and holding out a hand. Hollingsworth looked Violet up and down for a second before extending his own hand and shaking.

"Violet Despuis, you're the private detective. What

are you doing here?" he asked, the smile on his face leading to ice cold eyes.

"I have some questions to ask you about Amelia Waters," Violet said confidently, although the men around the table were now giving each other glances, wondering who this intruder was. "It is my understanding you were dating her."

"Well if that's your understanding, I won't deny it."

"Did you kill her?" Violet asked, and I saw a facial muscle in Hollingsworth's face twitch, although he managed to keep the smile in place.

"I did not," he replied.

"Where were you in the afternoon two days ago?"

"I was at the Queenwood Golf Club, enjoying a round with a few friends," he replied. "Not that I have to explain myself to you."

"Did you know about the program she was working on, the mathematical probability one?"

"Listen, Violet, I was dating Amelia, yes. And she was a nice girl. But I wasn't much interested in her maths skills, if you know what I mean. Now, look, I'm trying to have a nice breakfast here. I've answered your questions, now stop harassing me in front of my friends."

"All right, well, you say you did not kill her, so I will go," Violet replied, turning back toward the door. I noticed palpable relief among Hollingsworth's friends, but after Violet had taken three steps away, she stopped and turned back around. "But you know, I do have one more question. You are the kind of man who would prey on a naïve university student fresh from the country. You are the kind of man who would give her earrings and a handbag in exchange for her company, until eventually you pressure her into having sex with you, because you cannot attract a confident, young woman of the world on your own. What happened? Did she reject your advances? Did she tell you–rightfully–that purchasing her some expensive things did not give you the right to her body? Did you get angry, after having to ride a creaking lift which smelled of mildew up to her apartment?"

"How... how dare you?" Hollingsworth spluttered out, his face turning purple. "I'm one of the most powerful men in the country, I can have any woman I want. So I wanted to make a country girl happy for a little while. I can get along with anyone, regardless of class, I don't need to buy them things. So what if the lift in her building smells like mold. If you've ever been in a stable, you know that's nothing. I bought her those things to make her happy, to bring a bit of joy into her life. There were no strings attached and I certainly didn't kill her in anger."

Not only were the men at the table looking uncomfortable, but now after Hollingsworth's outburst, but now all other conversation in the room had stopped, as the other diners all looked toward the drama developing at the Hollingsworth table.

Violet simply laughed at him in return, and his face

turned another shade of purple. "Do you honestly believe that? That a brilliant young woman fell for a man like you, whose hair is starting to grey, because of your *charm*? That she would willingly let herself be groped by someone old enough to be her father?"

"Women like power," Hollingsworth growled at her. "And I have lots of power."

"You do! You have the power to buy sapphire earrings, and Balenciaga handbags. And I am certain that Amelia loved how the earrings glittered in the light in the selfies she took, even as she and her roommate giggled about how out-of-touch you are with her generation. I am not judging; after all, prostitution is the world's oldest profession, you were simply going about it in a legal way."

"That's enough!" Hollingsworth roared, stepping toward Violet and grabbing her violently by the arm.

"Be careful, please," Violet said, completely calmly. "I am rather fond of this arm, and do not want it to bruise. Just as I am sure you are rather fond of your nose being the shape it currently holds on your face."

A smile tugged at my lips as I realized Violet had just threatened the man.

"Oliver," one of the men at his table said quietly, and for a moment afterwards it was as though the world was standing still, until finally it was as though Oliver Hollingsworth realized what he was doing and let go of Violet's arm.

"I'm calling for security," he announced.

"It is all right, I can see myself out," Violet said to the man making his way toward her, and as she turned to the door she winked to the both of us, just as the waiter came by and put our food down in front of us.

I felt a little bit awkward. After all, should I go after Violet? Would that look weird? We were guests of Charles Dartmouth; would it be rude to leave him here? Luckily, a moment later Violet sent me a text.

Enjoy your breakfast with Charles, text me when you are finished and I will meet you outside.

"Now you know why I accepted Violet's invitation for breakfast," Charles laughed as he poured me some more tea. "You're welcome to go, of course, but if you'd like to stay I'd welcome your company."

"Of course I'll stay," I replied with a smile as I picked up my knife and fork. "Although I will admit to feeling slightly out of place here; medical school was expensive and my mom wasn't rich, so I was more used to take-out and cheap tacos than this sort of thing."

"Oh, well you're in better company than you would expect here," Charles told me. "The Athenaeum Club was originally created for the intellectual elite. This club has had members that have won Nobel Prizes in every category. Charles Darwin was a member here as well, among others. Having a brain and being able to use it is often more of an advantage here than being born into the right family."

"Unless your plan is to harass existing members in

STRANGLED IN SOHO | 85

the middle of breakfast, apparently," I replied with a small smile, and Charles laughed.

"Oh yes, well, I believe Violet will be quite chuffed for having been allowed to exit via the front doors after that stunt, but if she ever applied to be a member here there would no doubt be many who would second the motion. In fact, I wouldn't be surprised if a certain man's membership were revoked after that little scene, and I can't say I'll be displeased when it is," he added, and I realized then that Violet had goaded him into anger on purpose.

"She's really not worried about looking like an idiot in public," I said.

"Well, it's all in the pursuit of her murderer. I know all too well what lengths she goes to catch them. But you're a doctor, you say?"

"I didn't quite finish my degree. I got hit by a car six months before graduation so I can no longer be a surgeon."

"I'm sorry," Charles said. "That's a shame. I wondered about you since I saw you on the cover of *The London Post-Tribune* this morning with Violet."

"Oh yeah, that," I replied, my disgust for the paper evident in my voice.

"Eddie Cornwall is just upset that his boy's going to jail. Serves him right for letting the boy get away with anything and everything as a child. I can prove nothing, but let's just say this wasn't the first crime Edward

Cornwall Junior should have gone to prison for. He'll get over it."

"Well, it would be nice if he didn't rake Violet's name through the mud in the meantime."

Charles nodded thoughtfully. "Yes, it certainly would."

"Anyway, thank you for the lovely breakfast conversation," I said as our plates were cleared away.

"My pleasure," Charles replied, standing. He leaned over and did the double kiss on the cheek, but before pulling away, leaned close to me. "If you really want Cornwall to stop writing about Violet, I recommend that you do a bit of digging yourself. Perhaps look into the works of their star reporter, the one who wrote that article. He thinks wide, globally. You should too."

"Thank you," I replied, not entirely sure what Charles meant by that, but I'd spent enough time around Violet to know that way too many of her acquaintances spoke in riddles.

"Take care of yourself, it was nice to meet you."

"You too," I said, giving Charles a smile before turning and leaving the room, texting Violet on my way out that I was ready to meet back up with her.

CHAPTER 10

"*D*id Charles enjoy the show?" Violet asked me when I crossed the street after leaving the Athenaeum and met up with her.

"He did, he mentioned to me that Oliver Hollingsworth is likely to have his membership to the club revoked after that."

Violet grinned. "It was easier than I thought to provoke the man; control over one's emotions is one of the most important things in life, and Oliver Hollingsworth has none. Unfortunately for us, however, he did not kill Amelia Waters."

"How do you know that? Did you check his alibi?"

Violet shook her head. "There was no need. I mentioned the flatmate's name being Sarah, instead of Jessie, and that the building had a lift. He made no movement to correct me on the flatmate's name, which would by itself be understandable, but then he implied that he had been in the lift at Amelia's apartment. Of course, the building has none, which means that he has never been to Amelia Waters' apartment, where she was killed."

"Wow," I said, impressed. "That's some clever trickery."

"Thank you. Sadly, it does not get us any closer to our murderer, but I did not really believe Oliver Hollingsworth to have anything to do with it. I am convinced it was something to do with that maths program, it was not a personal situation. The man is a creep, that is certain, but he remains a creep who has likely not broken any laws in this particular instance, and he certainly did not murder Amelia."

"So, what do we do now?"

"We should go home. I need to think about this case. I need to figure out why someone would want the algorithm the four students were working on, and why they wanted it so badly they committed three murders to get it."

Violet hailed a cab and her brow furrowed as soon as we got in; she was obviously deep in thought.

As soon as the cab stopped in front of Violet's house, I hopped out of the car, Violet close behind me.

"Mind if I come in and use your computer?" I asked. After all, I wanted to look into that man Charles Dartmouth had told me about, and I figured using Violet's huge mac would be more comfortable than trying to get information on my iPad. Plus, I didn't want to be left out if Violet made any big breakthroughs this afternoon.

"Of course, come in," Violet replied, motioning toward the door. She unlocked it and stepped through the entrance, but as soon as she did, she stopped.

"Wait," she said to me, holding up a hand. "Do not come in, someone has been here."

I instinctively took a step back to find myself outside on the stoop. "Are you sure?" I asked, peering into the house, already knowing the answer. Violet was always right about these things, and she didn't bother answering me. Instead, she stepped inside the house carefully while I waited outside with bated breath. I was half expecting the house to be booby trapped Indiana Jones-style, and was prepared to duck if a giant fireball or something came through the front door.

"Ah, I found it," Violet said after about five minutes.

"Does that mean I won't die if I come in?" I called into the house.

"There are never any guarantees in life, but so far as I can tell, it is safe," Violet replied, and I stepped gingerly over the threshold and into the house, closing the door behind me.

Violet was sitting at the top of the stairs, looking carefully at the third step from the top. The stairs in her home were fairly modern: mahogany stained open risers with white closed stringers that gave the stairs a very open feel. I began to climb them to see what Violet was looking at, and she turned toward me, a small smile on her face.

"This is perhaps the best stroke of luck we have had all day."

"What's that?" I asked.

"Someone is trying to kill me."

"I'm pretty sure that's not the reaction normal people have in that sort of situation."

"Yes, well, normal people are boring."

"Normal people also tend to live longer."

"Only when they are not as good at my job as I am," Violet proudly announced. "Look under there, under that step. Be careful," she said, motioning to the step I'd been looking at. I bent down and contorted my body awkwardly to have a look. The underside of the step had a large crack in it. The next person to walk up the stairs would have fallen through the stair and fallen a good twelve feet onto the floor below, likely hitting their head on one of the adjacent steps on the way down as well.

"That wouldn't have ended well," I said.

"No, it would not," Violet replied. "It appears that somebody would like us to stop investigating the three deaths of the maths students."

"I'll call the police," I said, unlocking my phone, but Violet shook her head.

"Why bother? They will not do anything we cannot do better. It would just be a waste of time. Come. We will look at my security footage."

"How did you know something was wrong when we came in?" I asked as we walked down the stairs.

"One of my shoes by the door was a little bit sideways," Violet replied. "I am certain that they were straight when I left. Not only did I specifically notice it, but I would never leave my shoes tilted sideways."

"Who knew being incredibly neurotic would come in handy one day?" I teased as Violet turned on the computer.

She turned on the computer and the screen flashed to life; a minute later Violet opened a program and about six different security cameras popped up onto the screen, both from the interior and exterior of the house. One of them was pointed directly at us and I turned around, trying to see where it was hidden.

Eventually, through some trial and error, I found the camera hidden inside a vase sitting on a bookshelf. If I hadn't explicitly been looking for it, and didn't have a very, very good idea as to where it was, I never would have picked it as being a camera, I would have thought the small round lens was just part of the vase design.

"You should work for the NSA, they would love you," I told Violet.

"With the work that I do, it is both a good precaution to have such security, and it also comes in handy in situations like this, where we will be able to learn something about a potential murderer."

"If we're really lucky, he'll have had his home address printed on his shirt," I said.

"You would be surprised at how often people do wear clothes that absolutely gives them away," Violet replied as she moved the slider on the screen back to rewind the video. Everything was blank for a while until just after eleven in the morning, right around when we arrived at the Athenaeum Club, when a figure suddenly appeared on the tapes.

Violet slowed the video back down to real time and rewound it to the man's entrance and the two of us watched in silence.

The man first appeared in the video out the front of Violet's building, in the bottom right hand corner of the screen. He wore a baseball cap, with his head down that covered most of his face, along with a uniform– the kind a cable TV repairman would wear and a thin pair of black gloves which carried a small toolbox. It took him less than twenty seconds to pick the lock to Violet's front door, and I noticed her eyebrows raise just slightly. As he walked in our focus turned to the top center camera, pointing just inside the doorway. As soon as the man slipped into the door he turned away from the camera and replaced his cap with a balaclava; evidently, he was expecting Violet to have interior security cameras as well as exterior ones.

"Why don't you have some sort of security service here?" I asked Violet as the man turned back around to face us. His foot glanced against one of Violet's shoes as he made his way toward the stairs, knocking it askance.

"I get more information from people entering my

home if they stay here for a little while," Violet replied. "A security system would simply scare them off."

"I think that's the whole point, discouraging the person who's heading up your stairs to tamper with them."

"Well this way, we not only see what he is doing, we are learning more and more about him. For example, he is obviously a professional. He expected the security camera, and once inside, he replaced his cap with a balaclava. It is obvious from the way that he moves that he has done this before. He moves quickly, and confidently. He is not constantly looking over his shoulder. He is trained in carpentry, that much is obvious from the way he removed the step, tampered with it, and then replaced it. He has also injured his left shoulder at some point in the past. It appears to be quite stiff, and he makes a concerted effort to avoid using it when replacing the step."

As soon as the man finished tampering with the step, he made his way back down, then left out the front door the way he came. He replaced his balaclava with the baseball cap in the corner once again, ensuring we couldn't see his face from the camera angles, while at the same time making sure there would be no suspicion aroused by the neighbors.

"Wait," Violet said, pausing the video and looking intently at the screen.

"What?"

"What is that, do you think?" she said, pointing at

the man's neck. I squinted to look at where she was pointing. A part of the man's neck looked as though it was discolored.

"Birthmark?" I asked. "Unless he wanted a tattoo of an abstract blob for some reason."

Violet nodded. "Yes, I believe you are right. Give me one moment." She tapped away at the computer for a minute and the photo's quality enhanced. "Unlike some, I do not believe in half-rate security cameras," she said. Sure enough, my hypothesis was confirmed: the man had a small, port wine birthmark on his neck, about the size of a dime.

A small smile crept onto Violet's lips. "As soon as we find our killer, it will be very easy to confirm."

I nodded. This was definitely one of the best breaks we'd gotten in the case. "Did Peter Alcott make it onto his flight?" I asked, reminded of the man who was almost certainly a target now.

"Yes," Violet nodded. "I received an email from him a few moments ago, he is currently on a bus going from Venice to Ljubljana."

"Good. After all, I think this proves it: someone has been killing the people involved in this case, and they've been doing it in ways that make it look like an accident." Suddenly, my eyes widened. "Wait! That means that we're still not safe. Until we catch whoever did this, he's going to keep trying to come after us."

"Yes, he is," Violet nodded. "It would be a good idea if we were to fetch your cat from your flat, and have you stay here until this case is solved. After all, my house is much better prepared to handle attempts on our lives than yours."

I felt the blood draining from my face. People trying to kill me—whether on purpose or not—was getting really old.

CHAPTER 11

An hour later, Violet had come with me to get Biscuit. She was careful upon opening the door in case it was booby trapped, and insisted on doing a thorough search of my flat before we made our way back to her apartment, Biscuit, all of his necessary gear, and a quick bag packed with all my essentials and a few days' worth of clothes in hand.

"I will phone Mrs. Michaels sometime tomorrow," Violet said. "After all, if someone is trying to kill her tenant, she should be made aware of it."

"It'll give her time to advertise my apartment in the paper, at least," I deadpanned, and Violet cracked a smile.

"Do not be so pessimistic, our deaths would mean we were outsmarted by a criminal," she replied.

I couldn't think of anything witty to reply, but

luckily was saved from having to do so by the doorbell, whose dulcet tones rang through the house.

"Well, I really hope that's not the murderer," I said glibly as Violet got up to answer the door. A moment later I heard a familiar voice at the door; DI Carlson was here.

"Right, I've been told you've been tampering with evidence."

"I recommend not taking everything you hear at face value," Violet replied.

"So, you deny that you took Amelia Waters' laptop from her apartment?"

"Of course not. I did that, yes. I asked her room-mate's permission."

"Well, that laptop was evidence in a criminal inves-tigation. I need it."

"Well, you will have to say—how do you say in English—the magic word."

I snickered as I got up and made my way to the door. DI Carlson's face was already doing a great imitation of a ripe tomato, and he'd only been here for a few minutes.

"I should have you arrested!" he shouted, spittle flying from his lips.

"I would love to hear what crimes you believe I have committed."

"Impeding in a police investigation."

"Really? Because as I recall you telling me, Amelia Waters' death was not suspicious. So yes, I went to her apartment, and I took her laptop, but I made certain her roommate was aware of what I had done, so that it would not be difficult to find. None of that is a crime."

"Yes, well, it turns out the pathologist agreed with your incorrect assessment of what happened, and so now I'm being forced to investigate this suicide as though it were a murder."

A smile tickled my lips. "Oh no, you poor thing," I couldn't help but reply.

"Not you too," DI Carlson snarled my way. "Anyway, get me the laptop."

"I still haven't heard the magic word," Violet replied.

"I'm the police, I don't have to say please," he growled at her.

"I'm sorry, I did not realize your job title exempted you from the basic tenets of politeness," Violet replied. "As I am a private citizen, I also do not have to give you the laptop, I am perfectly within my rights to refuse, and have you get a warrant to retrieve it from my home."

I masked the peal of laughter that escaped me with a cough, and DI Carlson glared at me, then back at Violet. I knew she was being difficult because she found DI Carlson both lazy and annoying, and sure enough, eventually his lazy side won out.

"*Please* get me Amelia Waters' laptop," he snarled.

"Of course, it is just over here," Violet replied, making her way the ten feet to the desk where Amelia's closed laptop sat, grabbing the power cord as well and handing it to DI Carlson as though it was the easiest thing in the world. I kind of hoped he didn't have any heart troubles, because if he did I felt there was a good chance we were going to have to call an ambulance before he left.

"Stay the hell out of my investigation," he shouted at the two of us before turning on his heel and leaving without another word.

"He certainly made that more difficult than it had to be," I said to Violet, who laughed.

"Yes, the ones who think themselves to be so much smarter than the reality are the worst of the police inspectors. Detective Inspector Carlson would be a much better policeman if he learned a little bit of humility."

"So really you're just doing your part to improve his policing skills when you torment him like that."

"Of course," Violet replied. "Although I do not deny his quickness to anger is rather entertaining."

Biscuit wrapped himself around my feet just then, purring up a storm. I looked at the clock, it was three minutes after five.

"I'm sorry, am I three whole minutes late in giving you dinner?" I asked my kitty, who meowed as he walked to the kitchen, and I followed behind.

"So, what do we do about the case?" I asked Violet as I opened up a can of cat food.

"I do not know yet," Violet replied slowly. "We have some information about the murderer, but not enough to determine his identity. This case will not be as easy as that. I will spend tonight thinking about it. The mathematical algorithm Amelia and her group were working on is the key, I am certain of that."

I put some kibble out for Biscuit, who quickly began to eat it up, before sitting down at Violet's dining room table. She wandered back out toward the study to work on the case and I pulled out my phone. After all, I should at the very least let Jake know that I was going to spend the next few days at Violet's.

After a few false starts when it came to writing the text—how are you supposed to text your boyfriend that you're going to spend a few days at your friend's house because a homicidal maniac is trying to kill you?—I eventually settled on bluntness.

Amelia Waters' killer tried to kill us this afternoon, I'm going to spend a few days with Violet just to be safe, since her house is better set up to ward off killers than mine is.

I raided the fridge while waiting for a reply, eventually taking some nitrate free bacon, free-range eggs, fresh cheese, a red pepper and some spring onion—all organic, of course—and called out to Violet.

"Do you want an omelette for dinner?"

"That sounds delightful, thank you," she called back.

"Is anything in your fridge likely to send either one of us to the hospital?" I couldn't resist shouting back, and I heard Violet laughing from the couch in the study.

My phone pinged to indicate I'd gotten a reply text

just as I was putting the strips of bacon in the frying pan. Once they were on the heat, I made my way back to my phone.

Ok, sounds good, was all Jake replied. I furrowed my brow and re-read my original text. "Sounds good"? What kind of reaction was that to the fact that I had just told Jake there was a killer after me and Violet?

Really? You're not worried? I texted back. I chopped up the red pepper, perhaps with a bit more enthusiasm than I otherwise would have. Of course I didn't want Jake to panic or anything like that, but a little bit of concern would have been nice.

Sorry, he replied a minute later. *Rushed off my feet at the lab. Going to be here late again tonight. Please take care of yourself, Cass, and let me know if there's anything I can do for you. If there's a killer after you, honestly, I think being at Violet's is the best place for you.*

Thanks, I replied a moment later. *I think you're right. Things should be fine, hopefully Violet solves this case soon. Don't work too hard!*

When I didn't get a reply to that text I was a little bit disappointed, but I also completely understood. Although I never graduated to become a fully-fledged doctor, I had gone through medical school. I knew the hours could be ridiculous.

Still, as I piled the egg mixtures onto some plates along with bread I found in the cupboard that I was fairly certain was comprised entirely from bird seed, I couldn't help but feel a bit like Jake was pulling away from me right now. I wondered what was going on with him. Could he really just be super busy at work, or was there something else?

Unfortunately, right now, I had more pressing things to worry about than my budding relationship, like finding a murderer before he succeeded in killing us both.

CHAPTER 12

"*C*assie, wake up," I heard Violet hiss.

"Urrgh, go away," I muttered back sleepily, grabbing my pillow and shoving it over my face.

"It is important, wake up," Violet insisted, and as the previous day's events came flooding back to me I forced myself awake. What if the murderer was back?

"Ok, what is it?" I asked, as adrenaline coursed through my veins and sprang me into action even better than a cup of coffee could.

"I have uncovered a fairly major clue in our search for the killer. Come with me," she ordered, and I got out of bed, groaning as the knowledge that my murder was no longer imminent took hold, and that I had just been dragged out of bed to look at a clue.

"What time is it?" I asked as I followed Violet out of the guest room and down toward the stairs.

"I have no idea," Violet replied. When we got downstairs–carefully avoiding the broken step–I glanced at the old-fashioned clock on top of the mantelpiece and let out a groan.

"Did you seriously have to wake me up at three eighteen in the morning to look at a clue? Why aren't you in bed, anyway?"

"I could not sleep; anytime I closed my eyes I could only think of the algorithm and what someone could possibly want to kill three–possibly aiming for five–people for it."

"And did you figure it out?"

"I did," Violet exclaimed proudly. "And you will not believe what I have discovered."

"Ok, what is it?"

"Think about it. What sort of person needs to reverse a mathematical equation? Someone who is *trying to get into something.* For example, a safe." Violet's eyes were gleaming now, and mine widened as I realized where she was going with this.

"Oh!" I said.

"Yes, *exactement!* The day after Amelia Waters was killed, and her computer pilfered, a group of three men robbed a jewellery shop of millions of pounds worth of diamonds. This same group had robbed another diamond shop in the past as well, and a truck at the airport, but there was a difference: this time *they were able to enter the safe.*"

"So you think they stole the algorithm because it

would allow them to figure out the code to get into the safe?"

"*Oui, c'est ça.* In fact, I confirmed it only a few moments before waking you. I was able to get in touch with the owner of the store who was robbed–evidently he is having some difficulty in sleeping after what has happened–and he confirmed for me that the store's safe used a code which was changed automatically every twelve hours, with the resulting code sent via text message to his phone."

"So, if someone were to intercept those emails somehow, they could keep a record of them, and then using the algorithm Amelia and her friends came up with, figure out what the next code would be."

"*Précisement,*" Violet nodded. "In fact, I am certain that is what happened."

"But how can you know for sure that it was the same group of people? After all, it could have been a coincidence that they hit the diamond store the night after Amelia was murdered."

Violet motioned for me to look at the computer. "DCI Williams sent me the video files which he had promised to send, the ones of the diamond exchange robbery. Look for yourself."

I leaned over to look at the screen as Violet opened a video. Immediately the screen showed relatively grainy camera footage–it was better than your average gas station security camera, but I would have expected ultra-high definition from a jewellery place, to be honest—of the back room of the store.

For the first ten seconds or so of the video, there was no movement, but suddenly three figures, all dressed in black, wearing balaclavas, entered the screen. Violet was right when she had looked at the pictures and determined they were all professionals. One of the men immediately made his way to the safe and confidently typed in a series of numbers while the other two flanked him, looking around on either side, but without any panic. It was more like they were bodyguards than panicking robbers. As soon as the safe opened, all three men sprang into action. One man pulled out a Helly Hansen duffel bag, while the other two pulled out some old, ratty-looking backpacks. They immediately reached in and began pouring tray after tray of diamonds into the bags. When a jewel or two slipped out and onto the floor, the men didn't even react. Most of the gems, as far as I could tell, were loose stones; there were only a few in any settings, and they did grab a handful of watches as well. Just like with the previous robberies, they only went for the diamonds. The rubies, sapphires and emeralds left in the safe went ignored, as did a number of diamonds. Even in the grainy video I could see a *lot* of potential loot still left by the time they closed the safe and left.

Less than three minutes had passed in the video when the men closed the safe then confidently strode back toward what I assumed was the front of the store, out of view of the cameras.

"They definitely knew what they were doing," I said. "But I don't know if I recognized any of them."

"The man on the left, the one with the duffel bag. He was the man who came in here and attempted to kill us."

"Are you sure?" I asked, and Violet gave me that look that meant of course she was sure.

"There are exactly nine reasons why I am one hundred percent certain they are the same man, which range from the mannerisms, to the shoes he wore. I am absolutely certain that the man who attempted to kill us, and who killed Amelia Waters, is one of the Terrible Trio."

I couldn't help myself; even though this was incredibly dramatic, and a huge break in the case for us, I opened my mouth and yawned. I mean, to be fair, it was just after three in the morning. Exciting or not, I had the right to be pretty tired.

"So, what do we do now?" I asked.

"We will wait until morning, and we go see Mrs. Michaels, and then we will see DCI Williams. I believe that solving this case will be the fastest way to find our killer."

"Wait, how can Mrs. Michaels help?" I asked.

"Ah, she has more experience than most in these sorts of cases," Violet replied with a sly smile. "She may be old, but she is not nearly so innocent as she pretends to be."

I had a feeling there was more to Mrs. Michaels than met the eye, and I was looking forward to getting an opportunity to solve some of the enigma that was my landlady.

"Well, until then, I'm going to bed," I said, sleepily making my way up the stairs to the bedroom, only to find that Biscuit had moved into the warm spot on the bed I'd vacated.

"Move over, silly butt," I told my cat. "I haven't gotten up for the day just yet."

Biscuit let out a meow of protest as I had to pick him up and move him over to one end of the bed so that I could fit into the double as well. I laid my head down and fell asleep immediately.

However, with all the excitement of the night, the rest of my sleep was restless, and by the time six thirty rolled around I gave up completely and grabbed my iPad off the nightstand.

Remembering what Charles Dartmouth had said to me, I looked up the article on The London Post-Tribune from the previous day and found that it was written by one Keegan Coors. Scanning the article again made my blood boil; what he had written about Violet was practically slander.

I Googled his name and found that he had grown up in Greece, to a Greek mother and English father, before being shipped off to some posh boarding school, after which he got his journalism degree from Cambridge, which quite frankly I figured would in no way be able to match the ancient grandeur of Oxford. He got his start in journalism as a freelancer before being hired by *The London Post-Tribune*, where the owner Edward Cornwall took a keen interest in him and began to act as his mentor. He was now widely considered one of England's most prominent journalists.

I wondered what on earth it was that Charles Dartmouth wanted me to look at when it came to the man. He had told me to think globally. Maybe I should have started with Greece, then? But what did he want me to look at?

I thought about it for a minute. Charles had indicated that whatever Keegan had done, it was bad enough to be a big scandal. What kind of scandal could a journalist be involved in?

There was always the use of prostitutes, the old chestnut that had ruined many a political career, but not so much journalists. Plagiarism was the obvious one that came to mind, but there was also corruption. What if Coors was being paid off by someone in exchange for favorable or non-favorable articles being written in his paper?

I figured the best way to find out would be to start by going through Keegan Coors' old articles and seeing if anything stuck out. I typed his name into the search bar on *The London Post-Tribune*'s website and began to scroll through his article headlines.

It was obvious that Coors had been getting prime assignments to cover by the paper. His articles were largely comprised of the sort of thing that one would expect to see on the front page. *Grenfell Fire: Who's to Blame, Terrorist's Family Warned Police Before Attacks* and similar headline-worthy topics abounded.

There were a few that weren't quite so obvious, however. I clicked on one article that drew my eye: *Bank Purchase Deal Nearing Failure: Source.*

Now that was the sort of thing I could expect someone to get bribed over.

I opened the link and began to read.

Three months ago, the purchase of Central London Bank of Commerce *by the German Conglomerate* Bergen Gruppe *seemed all but certain. At the company's headquarters in Munich, the excitement in the air was palpable. The men and women—dressed in nothing but the best suits bought in Milan—walking through the glass-and-metal corridors that look more like they belong in a science fiction movie than the outskirts of the Bavarian capital have a noticeable spring in their step, and their enthusiasm and positivity make even the German language seem friendly and inviting. But as the deadline for the official signing of an agreement, which would make* Central London Bank of Commerce *one of the largest foreign-owned banks in the United Kingdom,* The London Post-Tribune *can reveal that sources close to the negotiation have let us know that those negotia-*

tions have stalled, and that a deal is unlikely to be completed at this time.

According to our sources, negotiations have stalled due to the current heads of Central London Bank of Commerce's *reluctance to agreeing to retirement terms for certain executives at the bank. Meanwhile, thousands of investors with the bank wait with bated breath to see if the deal will continue as planned, or if negotiations have stalled permanently.*

I leaned back against the bed and tried to think. There would be a lot of people who would want this deal to go through: I imagined most of the investors in the bank would. Usually buyouts like this came at a premium, affording healthy profits to investors. And going by the tone of the article, Keegan Coors was obviously pushing for the agreement to go through.

Just then there was a knock on the door.

"Cassie? Are you ready to go? We see Mrs. Michaels in ten minutes."

I put the iPad away, my mind whirring away as it considered what I'd just read. I was almost positive I was on the right track, now I just had to put the rest of the puzzle pieces together.

CHAPTER 13

It was just after seven thirty when Violet knocked on Mrs. Michaels' door. My landlady opened up a minute later, her arms opening wide when she saw us.

"Violet! Cassie! So lovely to see the two of you. Please, come upstairs, you must want some tea. Or perhaps something a little bit stronger? After all, the two of you are still young and this must be practically the crack of dawn for you. Not like me, when you get to my age, no one tells you the real reason we all get up so early is because we're afraid of missing any of the last few moments we have left on this earth."

I had to stifle a smile; Mrs. Michaels was definitely a personality.

"I will stick with the cup of tea, thank you," Violet said.

"Organic Herbal, as always?" Mrs. Michaels asked,

shuffling her way toward the kitchen after motioning for us to sit down on one of the couches in her living room.

"Yes, thank you," Violet replied, sitting.

"Something a bit stronger sounds good to me, thanks," I replied, eagerly anticipating the caffeine jolt from a cup of coffee. While my brain hadn't been able to sleep very well after my middle-of-the-night wake up call, that didn't mean it didn't have to.

"Of course, dear," Mrs. Michaels said. She came back a minute later with a pot of tea for Violet, then brought me over a mug of coffee. When I took a whiff, there came the unmistakable aroma of Bailey's, and I almost laughed out loud. Evidently when Mrs. Michaels said "stronger", she *meant* "stronger".

Sitting down across from us, she looked from one of us to the other. "So. What is it that brings you to my end of the street?"

"I am in need of information," Violet said. "Information which I am certain you will be able to provide."

"Pray, do tell," Mrs. Michaels asked, leaning forward. "Ever since Enid and Dorothy buried the hatchet after their feud over who gets to make Christmas sweaters using Sultan Blue colored wool there's been absolutely nothing exciting going on in my life."

"Wait, that was a feud?" I asked, and Mrs. Michaels turned to me.

"Oh, yes dear. And a rather nasty one at that. At one

point Dorothy called Enid's grandson's school and tried to have him expelled. It was quite entertaining, really, watching from the sidelines."

"I am certain that it was, but for now we require some information on a completely different matter," Violet said.

"Right. Of course. And what might that be?"

"The Terrible Trio. The diamond robbers. What do you know of them?"

"Well, as you know, I am but a kindly old lady now."

"Of course," Violet said deferentially, with a small smile on her face. Wait, *this* was what we were here to talk to Mrs. Michaels about? Jewellery theft? And she was a good source of information about it?

"I may have heard a few details here and there. Although, to be perfectly honest, I'm quite surprised at how quiet this latest group has been. There has been virtually no chatter among those with whom I keep in regular contact about identities, or process, or where they plan on hitting next."

"Now that is interesting," Violet said quietly. "What do you know?"

"I know that they only steal diamonds. And they move around a fair bit; they've only hit one shop in Hatton Garden."

"What's Hatton Garden?" I asked.

"It is the London jewellery center," Violet replied. "Equivalent to your diamond district in New York City."

"So, two of their three hits have been outside of Hatton Garden, which is interesting in and of itself, since most major thefts take place there. But I must say, there is a certain finesse to these crimes. Back in my day–er, should I say, my husband's day–there was no finesse to the crime. He would run in, smash some cases, grab some jewellery, and that was that. He was in and out, and a few tens of thousands of pounds richer. But these crimes–they are beautifully done. Reading about them is like seeing a work of art. Whereas my husband's crimes were those of a jackhammer, smashing away at everything, these are the work of a scalpel. They are precise, and perfect, and they come out of each robbery with the kind of money my husband could only dream of."

I took a sip of my Bailey's coffee to hide my pure surprise. So, Mrs. Michaels' husband had been a jewellery thief?

"You mean your husband stole jewellery?" I asked, unable to resist the question that had been on my lips all the same.

"Oh yes, dear," Mrs. Michaels said. "Of course, he wasn't my husband at first. We were just lovers when he started out. It was the sixties, after all. What was a little bit of crime to help overthrow the capitalist system?"

"Do not pretend that you were *completely* innocent, Mrs. Michaels," Violet replied with a small smile.

"Well I may have taken part in a spot of smuggling

here and there, but what's sneaking a few hundred thousand dollars' worth of diamonds across the channel to Antwerp between friends?"

Of course Mrs. Michaels would consider that "a spot" of smuggling. At this rate, I was going to need another shot of Bailey's in my coffee.

"Now," she continued, "I do think that whoever is doing this has some experience with a lot of things. You say there are three men?"

Violet nodded.

"Well in that case, they are almost all specialized in some way. One thing that is curious about this case is that this last robbery is the first one where they entered a safe. They are getting more sophisticated with every hit. The first one was the closest thing they have committed that could be called a smash-and-grab, in the middle of the day. Nothing too fancy about that, except that even then they were very well organized."

Mrs. Michaels paused, then continued. "They had an exit strategy. They were not like those idiots a few years ago who fled on mopeds and were stopped by a crowd who had noticed the robbery; they were in and out without anyone outside of the store staff noticing anything was wrong.

"The second time, they targeted a truck at Heathrow airport carrying diamonds to cargo to Dubai. That was a much smoother operation, but also so much more daring. After all, with airport security the way it is these days, can you imagine how much work must have gone into ensuring they weren't caught? And this last one, in which they managed to break into a safe in four minutes and get out, is even better. Your thieves are fast learners; they are improving with every score."

"Which would imply that they are new to the game, no?" I asked.

"New, perhaps, yes. Or they are recent transplants to England, with experience overseas. If they are new to the robbery game, they are hands down the best beginners I have ever seen."

Violet nodded slowly. "And yet you have heard nothing about their identities."

"Nothing concrete, no. There have been rumours that one of them might be a foreigner, but I've heard nothing really solid or even really reliable. It really does feel like they're ghosts. I mean, even back in seventy-one, when the Baker Street robbery happened and there were calls of D-notices being sent out and rumors of the police trying to quash any information about that robbery, everyone knew the car dealer who was behind it all. My husband was even involved in helping him get out of the country after."

"Wait, is that the robbery that they ended up making a Jason Stratham movie about? The one where they robbed a place just to hide some pictures of the royal family?" I asked, and Mrs. Michaels turned to me.

"Oh yes, that was it," she said with a small smile. "Although by all accounts from those of us who were around at the time, the film took *significant* liberties when it came to the facts. They did get that one right though; compromising pictures of Princess Margaret were in fact the real reason that robbery happened."

I shook my head slightly. These were events *movies* had been made from, and my eighty-something year old landlady knew all about them. Evidently there was much more to Mrs. Michaels than I could have ever imagined.

"I'm sorry I can't be more useful to you," Mrs. Michaels said. "I would tell you who they were if I knew."

"Thank you anyway," Violet said to her. "The fact that you have heard nothing is telling in and of itself."

"I'll put the feelers out to some of my contacts all the same," she replied. "You never know what might come up."

"Thank you," Violet replied. "But do not go to too much trouble on my behalf. These men are not only robbers, they are murderers as well. So far, they have killed three people, and they have attempted once to kill me. I do not doubt they will make another attempt on both my life and Cassie's, so she is staying at my house for a few days."

"Violet, you do realize I didn't get well into my eighties without a little bit of sense about me, do you not? And should my decision to meddle in your affairs result in my death, well, I've had a good, long life and we've all got to go sometime."

"If you die, you cannot supply me with any more information in the future, so I would greatly appreciate it if you did your best to remain on this earth all the same," Violet replied.

"Well, how can I deny you after such an emotional outburst?" Mrs. Michaels replied, and I laughed.

"Now, if you will excuse us, Cassie and I are now on a little bit of a timetable, as we need to find out the identity of these men—well, one of them at least—before he succeeds in killing us."

"Oh don't pretend like he even has a chance of succeeding," Mrs. Michaels replied. "Though I'd be willing to wager that this will be the most difficult robbery you've ever had to solve."

"We will see," Violet said. "I hope not, personally. I had one take me three years before I finally caught the perpetrator, and I would rather not have to actively watch for an assassin for that long this time."

"All the best, anyway. Let me know what you find out," Mrs. Michaels said as she led us to the door. "And Cassie, if you would ever like to hear some of the stories of my past, please feel free to come up anytime, and let it be known that I am very much a fan of those biscuits you made that one time, and of merlot," she added with a wink.

"I will absolutely come by soon then," I replied, and I meant it. Especially if it meant sharing a batch of cookies with Mrs. Michaels. Right now, however, assassin or not, there was nothing I wanted to know about more than her past after this conversation. I felt like my head was still spinning, and it was nothing to do with the alcohol I'd just ingested, even though it wasn't even nine in the morning yet.

CHAPTER 14

"Right, you all have your assignments. Off you go. Let's get these men," DCI Williams said to the crowd of thirty-odd police officers of varying rank in front of him at Paddington Green police station as Violet and I walked into the room. I almost did a double-take when I saw him; he looked like he'd aged about five years since I saw him last, about twenty-four hours ago.

As the group of officers dispersed, mostly in small groups, chatting to one another about their assignments for the day, DCI Williams spotted us, and the relief on his face was immediately apparent. Bags under his eyes and what appeared to be an extra line of wrinkles and a few more greying hairs made it obvious that this case was taking its toll on him.

"Thank God," he said when he saw Violet, any semblance of official self-confidence completely gone.

This was a man who was obviously desperate. "Please tell me you got a chance to look at the videos I sent you."

"It is your lucky day," Violet replied. "One of the men you seek also happens to be the murderer I am after. I did look at your videos."

"And do you know who did it?"

"Unfortunately, even I am unable to tell so far. However, I can tell you that one of the men you are looking for has a small port wine birthmark on the back of his neck."

"I'll make sure that goes out in the next internal release in an hour," DCI Williams said, typing furiously into his phone.

"I am here because I need access to all of your files on the previous robberies, and I want to go to the scene of the most recent theft," Violet announced.

DCI Williams didn't protest at all, he just nodded. "Sure, whatever you need. Let me grab you those files."

About two minutes later Violet and I were sitting at his desk, going through the files on the other two robberies committed by the Terrible Trio. Violet was going through their first robbery, a daylight smash-and-grab, while I read about the second robbery, in which the trio of thieves managed to hijack a truck carrying over ten million pounds worth of uncut diamonds heading for a cargo plane going to Dubai. It was one of the largest diamond heists in UK history.

The whole story was really quite incredible. The

diamonds were scheduled to travel on a British Airways flight from Heathrow to Dubai, in the cargo hold. The three men were able to fake credentials to get onto the airport tarmac and hijack another truck. They caught up to the truck carrying the diamonds and forced the men driving the truck out at gunpoint. What happened afterwards is still a mystery: the truck never made its way back onto security camera screens, but was eventually found abandoned on the grounds of Heathrow Airport, the uncut diamonds gone, and no sign of the three men who had stolen them.

There was surprisingly little security camera footage of the men. Like in all their thefts, they seemed to have mastered the art of avoiding security cameras wherever possible, and the few camera images there were simply showed men with caps covering their faces, heads down away from the cameras, wearing British Airways uniforms.

It was strange, looking at the image of a man I knew had broken into Violet's home and sabotaged her step to make her death look like an accident. I shivered, knowing how easily I could have been the one going up the stairs in her house as well.

I shook my head as I read through the statements from the men driving the truck which had been stolen. By the time they were hijacked, the three men had put on masks, so their faces weren't seen. They barked out single words, rather than sentences, presumably to make it more difficult to recognize their voices, and they knocked the men unconscious almost immediately and placed them in the truck they had taken on the tarmac to maximize the amount of time they would have to get away without anyone noticing anything.

I had to admit, it seemed like an almost perfectly planned crime. And I supposed in a way it was, seeing as the men hadn't been caught, and the diamonds were all in the wind.

As Violet let out a grunt of frustration, I figured that the first robbery left equally few clues.

"Not as easy as you expected to solve this?" I asked Violet, passing her over the file I'd just finished reading. After all, I wasn't getting any new information from it.

"I must admit, these men are good. They have the best qualities for a group of robbers: they are patient, and they are organized. It took them *months* before they managed to get the algorithm by killing Amelia Waters. I imagine that for whatever reason they were not able to get it when they killed the first two students, but they did not act in haste. They waited until they had the algorithm to commit the third robbery, and they did so swiftly and successfully. The details are different but even the first robbery was the same. It was organized. The men had obviously put thought into it. The only similarity between all of the crimes is that diamonds are the target."

"So how are you going to solve it? Not to give you a spoiler alert or anything, but the second robbery is pretty much the same as the most recent one: as far as I can tell there's nothing in the file that can help us find the suspects."

"There is never *nothing*," Violet said with a small smile as she opened the file and looked through it. "I do not yet know how we will solve this case. But for now, we continue to read the information we have, and then we go to see where the last robbery took place."

She motioned for DCI Williams to come over; he had been talking to one of his coworkers in the corner while Violet had commandeered his desk for her investigations.

"I want to see the location of the theft," she said, and DCI Williams nodded.

"Of course. Come with me, I'll drive you there."

As we walked past the multitude of cops, I saw more than a few of them giving both of us nasty looks. Violet wasn't exactly one of the cops' favorite people in London; she had a tendency to think most of them were idiots, and they weren't exactly appreciative of the fact that she pointed it out on a regular basis.

"What's she doing here, doesn't Williams think we can handle this?" I heard one man ask the woman next to him.

"Right," DCI Williams said suddenly, loudly, stopping in the middle of the room. He turned to face the officers that were still around. "Those of you who know me know that Violet Despuis and I get along well enough. And yes, I have brought her in on this investigation. The fact is, these men have committed three successful robberies, show no intent to stop, and we're not getting anywhere fast. So yes, I've brought in an outsider. No matter what you think of her, she knows how to do the job, and she does it pretty well. If I hear any complaining about the fact that she's helping us solve this crime, you can consider yourself off this task force. Because quite frankly, none of you should be complaining that I'm doing what I have to do to solve this case. Got it?"

A low grumbling murmur of reluctant assent passed through the crowd. DCI Williams turned and we continued to leave the room. I smiled to myself; I knew all too well that DCI Williams' announcement wouldn't have changed anyone's opinion about Violet, but might just have changed how they acted in front of her with the boss around.

"You must have made a good impression somewhere, to now be in charge of an entire task force on your own," Violet told DCI Williams as he motioned for us to get into an unmarked police car, a brand new BMW 3-series.

"Yes, I think so," DCI Williams confirmed. "In fact, I believe if I manage to solve this case I'll be up for a promotion to superintendent soon."

"Ah, then I believe congratulations are in order! I am certain you will be able to crack this case."

For a man who should have been thrilled about an upcoming promotion, DCI Williams certainly didn't act like it. Instead of accepting Violet's congratulations, he sighed. "Do I really deserve it, though? I mean, let's be honest: a lot of the high profile cases I've solved have been thanks to you. I never would have solved so many of my cases without you. There was that serial killer a few years back, and then the man who tried to fake his own death for the insurance money. And of course, that quadruple murder just this year, and that bombing in Belgravia just after that. I got the credit for it, but it was really thanks to you that they got solved at all."

"You do not give yourself enough credit," Violet replied. "I have no illusions about myself and my methods: I am not always an easy person to get along with, particularly not with those of limited intelligence, which, quite frankly, describes a large portion of the Metropolitan Police Service. However, despite this, unlike your peers you have recognized that I am still able to bring value to your cases, and you work with me all the same. There is something to be said for recognizing someone who is superior to you and using their work in order to further a common goal. And the fact that you have been able to do that is why you are being considered for the promotion, whether it is because of my own superior investigative skills or not."

"Wow, that's the closest thing to a compliment I think you've ever given him!" I exclaimed, and DCI Williams laughed as he pulled the car away from the curb.

"While there was a bit of self-congratulation in that speech, I understand your point," he said. "Thank you."

"There was no self-congratulation at all, only fact," Violet replied as we sped through central London to Oxford Street, and I hid a smile.

CHAPTER 15

A few minutes later we found ourselves driving down one of the most glamorous shopping streets in all of London. To our left was the huge Selfridges department store, whose whitewashed walls were lined with Corinthian columns built into the walls while flags from around the world flittered in the light wind above the building.

As DCI Williams deftly drove around red double decker busses and small black taxi cabs, he parked on the right-hand side of the street, where flagship stores lined the street level as shoppers meandered slowly through the crowds, savoring not only their purchases, but the entire shopping experience.

It being central London, there were absolutely no parking spots nearby, so DCI Williams parked the car in a "no parking" zone on a side street across from the

French Connection flagship store, putting police ID on the dashboard so it wouldn't get towed.

Leading us across the street, we made our way to a shop that was small, but obviously high class. The window advertised them as being a dealer of Patek Philippe watches, and other high-end jewellery. If it weren't for the fact that the shop had been in the news every day since the robbery, one would be hard-pressed to know a robbery had even taken place.

The three of us made our way up to the white-walled exterior, with floor-to-ceiling glass windows, and DCI Williams opened the door to allow us to make our way inside.

Violet stayed outside for a few moments longer, looking at the exterior of the building while the two of us entered. There were three customers in the store: a man in a business suit who looked harried while being shown women's watches–I suspected he'd forgotten an important anniversary and was now making up for it, a well-dressed woman sitting on a stool while examining stones offered to her by a short, nervous-looking man, and a third man who looked at the small display of watches while waiting his turn to be served.

The man showing the watches looked up and saw DCI Williams enter, with me behind him, and I immediately noticed the displeasure in his face. I wasn't sure if it was because we obviously weren't customers–although I didn't think I was dressed *that* badly–or because he was tired of having the police around all the time. As he excused himself and motioned for us to come over to a corner of the store, just as Violet entered and joined us, I discovered it was the latter.

"How much longer are you people going to harass me?" he asked. "I understand you've got a job to do, but so do I, and having the police about every other day isn't good for business." Just then, the man who had been patiently looking at the display left the store, and the store's owner motioned toward the door. "See? You're driving away my customers."

"Simon, I understand your frustration, but we have a job to do. We're trying to recover your diamonds that were stolen."

"Recover? Ha. I know just as well as everyone else that those diamonds are lost forever. You haven't caught the Terrible Trio yet, and I saw the security footage as well: there's nothing there that will help you find them."

"Apart from the fact that one of the men has an old shoulder injury, you must mean," Violet said coldly. "You are a jeweller. I do not pretend to tell you which diamond to recommend to someone, you should not pretend to tell us what can and cannot be gleaned from evidence."

The owner, Simon, looked over at Violet with dislike. "And who is this?"

"This is Violet Despuis, you might have heard of her. She's helping with the investigation."

"You're the one who put that newspaper owner's kid in jail," Simon replied.

"Technically it was the Crown Prosecutor who did that, although I was instrumental in gathering the evidence to allow him to do it, yes," Violet replied.

Simon nodded. "Fine. Look around, do what you want. Here's the key to the back room," he said, handing Violet a set of keys. "I'm going back to my customer. Try not to be too intrusive."

Violet smiled. "He is not going to like what I am about to do next. Please, go into the back area, and start a timer exactly thirty seconds after the door closes behind you. I want to time how long it will take me to get in."

"All right," DCI Williams said, obviously not completely sold on the fact that this was a good idea. He took the keys from Violet and the two of us went to the thick door at the back, unlocking it and making our way inside.

The back room was spacious, but scattered. A large desk filled the left-hand side of the room, covered with papers. To the right was the safe, I recognized it from the video. It was bolted to the wall behind, four feet tall, with security cameras on the wall above pointing directly toward it.

"All right, time," DCI Williams said as the door closed behind us, and he looked at the timer on his phone. After thirty seconds, he started it again.

It took just over a minute before Violet opened the door and came inside.

"Sixty-four seconds," DCI Williams announced, and Violet frowned.

"The men were slightly faster than me," she replied. "Whoever their lockpick is, he is very good."

"Is that your yardstick to measure by?" I asked. "Whether or not someone is better than you at picking locks?"

"It is a great measurement tool," Violet said. "I am without a doubt in the top zero point one percent in the world at this skill. For someone to be even better at it than me is exceptional."

DCI Williams grinned, but I had to admit, Violet's reasoning was sound. "Now, let us look at this safe."

The three of us made our way over. The lock on it was old school, the type that you had to turn in a circle multiple times and stop on the right number.

"This is a Pandora Six-Thousand," Violet said as she looked carefully at the safe, making sure not to touch anything. "They are custom made and advertised as being one of the safest vaults available for high-end jewellery shops. Note that there is no number pad; that is so that the record of the numbers touched cannot be determined. However, despite the old-style exterior, there is a lot of technology in this machine. The code to enter is changed every twelve hours, and is sent via text message to a pre-determined phone number. How our thieves were able to access a number of those text messages, I am not quite certain yet. The vault is completely tamper-proof, and contains a seismic detector, so that any attempt at drilling through the vault will immediately trigger an alarm. As far as I am aware, no one until now had successfully managed to break into this vault before."

"Don't tell me that means you're going to give it a shot too," I said, and Violet shot me a rueful smile.

"Alas, no. We do not have the algorithm with us, nor do we have the data available to allow us to use it to crack this safe. We will need Simon for that."

"I'll go and get Simon to come back here and open the vault."

A minute later the jeweller walked into the back room. "I've left my son alone out there with the customers, but if it gets busy he'll have to call me back out," Simon warned.

"That is fine," Violet said. "Please, go about opening this safe the way you would any other day. Do not do anything differently."

Simon strode over to the locked vault, took his phone from his pocket, took a pair of reading glasses from his pocket and put them on, then after presum-ably reading the code to open the safe, he put the phone down and turned the dial on the vault four times. There was a click, and he opened the vault door.

I could see handfuls of diamonds, rubies, emeralds, sapphires and a few expensive watches glimmering inside the vault. There had to be at least a hundred thousand pounds' worth of jewellery in there, on top of everything in the display cases outside.

"When does the code for the vault change?" Violet asked him.

"Six every morning, and six at night," Simon replied without hesitation.

"Do you look at the code every day?"

"Only the morning code. I get here a little bit after seven, so I need it to get into our stock for the day, and by six it's always off the floor and put back in the safe. I always get the text with the night time code, but I'm home by then and usually don't even bother looking at it. I try to keep away from my phone after work hours, until I go to bed and set my alarm, anyway."

Violet nodded slowly. "Do you wear your glasses at night, when you set that alarm?"

"No, I can usually stumble my way through that part of my routine," Simon said. "Although I don't understand what this has to do with the robbery."

"Well I do, and that is what is important. Now, the pen you have in your pocket, can I look at it?"

"This thing?" Simon asked, handing Violet a Mont Blanc pen engraved with the initials S.R. that had been in his shirt pocket.

"*Oui*, that," Violet replied, taking the pen from him and examining it closely. "Do you wear this in your pocket all the time?"

"Yes, I do," Simon replied, looking at DCI Williams, as if for an explanation as to why the famous detective

Violet Despuis wanted to know about his pen. A moment later, she smiled in triumph.

"I believe we know now how the thieves got data from the machine," Violet said, unscrewing the cap from the pen and examining it closely. "If you look carefully, just above the pen clip, you will notice a tiny camera built into the cap, made to mimic this pen exactly."

I took the pen cap from Violet and squinted at where she'd mentioned. Sure enough, by looking super closely, in the right light, the tiniest glint of a lens became visible.

"So that was how they found out the code!" Simon wailed. "That means whoever did this must have been in my shop. I must have let him use my pen."

Violet nodded. "Yes, that is most likely. I would suspect that it was done months ago, and that the thieves have been collecting the data ever since as they attempted to gain access to the algorithm the Oxford students were working on."

"So now we know the how, we just don't know the who," I said.

"Yes, but more importantly, we do not know the *why*," Violet said.

"What do you mean?"

"The other two robberies were executed just as well as this one, and their take at both previous robberies was far superior. Here, they left a number of watches and jewels in the safe. It is not as though they were in a rush; they had not been caught and they were obviously professional enough to not panic. They had plenty of time to get in and out. They had disabled the alarm system. Why did they leave so many jewels here? That is what I want to know."

"Maybe they were worried someone would see them?" Simon ventured a guess.

"No. These were not the type to worry. They closed the roller shutter after entering, and I guarantee you that they ensured no one saw them enter. These were not the kind of men to do things badly. There is something else at work here. Anyway, I think I have seen enough here for now. Come, Cassie, we will go home for now."

"I'll drop you off at home," DCI Williams said. "Saves you the fare on a taxi, and I want to talk to someone I know in Kensington anyway."

We left the jewellery store, and to be honest I kind of felt like we'd uncovered more questions than we had when we walked in. It seemed like we were even further away from solving Amelia Waters' murder.

CHAPTER 16

When we got home, Violet said she was going to spend some time in the study, thinking about the case. I excused myself to my room, making sure to step over the still-broken stair, and picked up my iPad once more. I decided to try and dig a little bit further into the newspaper case. After all, if I could prove that Keegan Coors had been bribed to write an article, I would... well, to be honest I wasn't really sure what I would do. I'd figure it out when I got there. But surely I could use it as leverage somehow to make the paper stop writing nasty things about Violet, right?

I started off by Googling the name of the German firm that was attempting to purchase the London Bank of Commerce: Bergen Gruppe.

Of course, most of the articles I came across were in

German, but thanks to Google Translate that wasn't much of an issue. From reading a few articles, it quickly became apparent that Bergen Gruppe was one of the largest banking conglomerates in Germany. Not content with sticking within their borders, they had spent the last five years aggressively expanding internationally: they now owned major banks in Austria, Slovenia, Croatia, Greece, Italy and Spain, and on top of the current deal they had in the works with the London Bank of Commerce, they were also in negotiations with two banks in Portugal.

The Euro values involved in these deals were absolutely mind-boggling.

English-language articles that I read about the deal seemed to be evenly split as to whether or not the deal was a good idea. Some lauded the fact that the English banking giant would be able to remain solvent after being acquired by the German company, as they were hit hard during the recession of 2008. Others bemoaned the idea that a London icon would move into foreign hands.

Of course, *The London Post-Tribune* seemed to be part of the latter group, with most of their opinions written about the merger being critical rather than praising.

I didn't really know how else to go about looking for information, so I decided to see what other countries thought about the merger. I created a list of the banks that had been taken over by Bergen Gruppe and began to read articles written in those languages. In Slovenia, the reception seemed pretty positive, and I couldn't find any recent articles written about it that were negative toward the idea. In Greece, however, the sentiment was strongly opposed.

Using Google Translate, I read through one article describing the merger:

At the headquarters of the company in Munich, the enthusiasm in the air was visible. Men and women-who did not wear anything other than the best costumes they bought in Milan-walk through the glass and metal corridors that look more like science fiction movies than the outskirts of the Bavarian capital have a remarkable source in the footsteps. Their enthusiasm and positivity make even the German language friendly and welcoming. As the deal is to be confirmed on Wednesday, it seems obvious now that nothing will stop this German company from owning one of the largest Greek banks.

Ok, so Google Translate still wasn't the best. Still, as I read the translation, I frowned to myself. Something about that Google translation seemed really familiar. It was like I'd read it before. In fact, I was almost certain that I had. My brow furrowed in concentration as I typed away on the iPad, my excitement growing. Maybe I'd been all wrong about this after all. Maybe Keegan Coors wasn't being paid to tank the deal in the press. Maybe Keegan was plagiarising his articles!

About three minutes later I managed to find the

article I'd been looking at. Sure enough, it read almost word-for-word the same way as the article in the Greek newspaper:

At the company's headquarters in Munich, the excitement in the air was palpable. The men and women – dressed in nothing but the best suits bought in Milan – walking through the glass-and-metal corridors that look more like they belong in a science fiction movie than the outskirts of the Bavarian capital have a noticeable spring in their step, and their enthusiasm and positivity make even the German language seem friendly and inviting.

I had him! This had to be what Charles Dartmouth was talking about. And what he meant when he said to look globally. Keegan Coombs was getting away with plagiarism by directly translating works from Greek papers. After all, his mother had been Greek, he probably grew up speaking in Greek with her. It wouldn't be a stretch to imagine that she taught him to read her mother tongue as well.

Just then, my phone pinged next to me. It was a text from Jake, asking me if I wanted to hang out.

Can't right now. Busy. Talk later, I texted back quickly. I felt a little bit bad; it felt like I hadn't seen Jake in forever, but really it had only been a few days. Maybe it was the fact that the last time I'd seen him was when I was at the hospital that made it seem worse than it really was.

"Violet," I called out as I made my way down the

stairs, remembering to avoid the tampered step at the last moment.

"*Oui?*" she replied. She was lying upside down on the couch in the study, her legs draped over the back of the couch as her hair fell to the floor. She looked up–well, down, I supposed–at me, questions in her eyes.

"What… are you doing?" I asked, looking at her.

"I am thinking in a position which maximizes the blood flow to my brain, stimulating me through both the increased blood flow and also by changing my perspective on a scene that I see on a regular basis. But surely that is not the question you have come to ask."

"No, uh, I need to know where I'd go to find someone that speaks Greek."

"Palmers Green, in North London if you are looking for a Greek speaker in general. If you require the services of someone closer to home, go to the gyro place on Gloucester Road. Ask for Ioannis, tell him Violet sent you. He will tell you anything you need to know."

"Wow… thanks," I said. Gloucester Road was only a few minutes' walk away, and knowing someone specific was going to be a lot easier than asking random Greek-looking strangers if they could help me figure out if someone was plagiarising someone else.

"It is not a problem. Now, go. I am thinking."

As I left the front door I waved at Mrs. Michaels, who was in her garden, and did a double take when I realized what I originally thought were clippers was actually a machete. She waved at me with her gardening gloves, the smile under her wide-brimmed straw hat making her look so innocent that I almost doubted myself for a minute until I saw the long blade gleaming in the sun.

It appeared Mrs. Michaels was definitely ready for anything the murderer had planned for Violet and me.

Shaking my head slightly–but at the same time being a bit thankful Mrs. Michaels was there, just in case–I made my way toward Gloucester Street, my iPad in hand. I actually knew exactly which small Greek hole-in-the-wall Violet was talking about, I'd eaten gyros there a few times and had to say, they were pretty good.

When I got to the counter, the young man working greeted me with the kind of smile and hello that I knew he saved for the locals he recognized.

"What can I get for you today?" he asked, leaning against the counter. My mouth watered as I looked at the standard pictures on the wall, but knew that I was here for something else. "Maybe in a bit, I was told to come here and talk to Ioannis," I said.

"Sure thing," he nodded. "Dad! Come out here, there's someone who needs to speak to you!"

A minute later the man's father came out. Wearing a stained apron that bulged over his belly, with a balding head and a friendly face, Ioannis made his way toward me.

"Hello there," he told me, shaking my hand. He still

had the smallest hint of a Greek accent when he spoke, but had obviously been in England for a long time. "Looking for a job, are you?"

"Um, no," I replied. "Violet Despuis sent me here, she told me that you'd be able to translate some Greek for me."

Ioannis laughed. "But of course! Anything for a friend of Violet. What can I do for you?"

I opened the documents where I had copied and pasted the stuff that I suspected was plagiarized, and showed them to Ioannis.

"I need to know if the English and the Greek in these files essentially say the same thing. Would they be considered plagiarism?"

Ioannis' eyes scanned the page quickly. He muttered to himself as he read, and then looked up at me.

"Yes, these translations are good. I would say the English and the Greek works are identical."

My suspicions were officially confirmed by a source far more reliable than Google Translate. Keegan Coors had been plagiarising works from Greek newspapers and passing them off as his own.

"Thank you!" I said to Ioannis. "Thank you so much!"

"Not a problem. A friend of Violet's is a friend of mine. Come back to see me anytime if you have more questions, if we are open, I am here."

"I will, thanks," I said, my excitement making me giddy.

As I walked back home, a delicious chicken gyro in hand, I knew that I had exactly the information that I needed to make sure Keegan Coors and *The London Post-Tribune* stopped writing lies about Violet. And I'd figured it out all by myself! Well, almost, anyway.

CHAPTER 17

When I got back home, Violet was still lying on the couch in the same position. Now, however, Biscuit had found out about it and was currently entertaining himself by pouncing on Violet's hair as it lay on the floor.

"Stop it, let her think," I scolded my cat, picking him up off the floor as he let out a meow of displeasure.

"It is all right, he was not bothering me," Violet said.

"Not yet, anyway. Cats are weird. One minute they're innocently playing with your hair, the next they're doing the same thing with your scalp. Trust me, I probably just saved your life."

Violet laughed as she sat up. Biscuit was now perched on my shoulder, looking down at the last piece of chicken in my gyro. I sighed, picked it out of the wrap and handed it to him, and he happily ran off toward the kitchen with the chicken in his mouth.

Smiling after my cute little cat, I crumpled the empty wrapper as Violet sat up.

"Was Ioannis able to help you with your Greek problem?"

"He was, thanks for recommending him," I said. I didn't want to explain to Violet what I'd discovered. After all, I knew that if she knew I was trying to get a newspaper to stop printing lies about her, she would just tell me not to worry about it, and that she'd had lies printed about her numerous times before.

This was my solution to the problem, and my solution alone.

Luckily for me, before Violet had a chance to answer any more questions, there was a ring at the front door.

"Ah!" Violet exclaimed. *"Très bien!* That will be Andrew, he is a carpenter that I have hired to fix the step for us. Finally, we will no longer have to watch our step when we go up the stairs," she said happily, making her way to the front door.

I couldn't help but notice she looked through the peephole just to be sure before she opened the door wide and greeted him.

"'*Allo*, Andrew, how are you?"

"Violet," the man in front of her replied, breaking out into a grin. "How have you been?"

"Well, someone has tampered with one of my steps in an attempt to kill me, and my friend Cassie, but apart from that things have been fine. How about yourself?"

"Well, Jenny's pregnant again," he replied, running a hand through his ginger hair. He was about six feet tall, and built like a tradesman, with that muscular look that obviously came more from hard labor than from the gym.

"Congratulations, my dear!" Violet said. "Come, come, let me show you the step."

Andrew nodded to me with a smile as Violet led him toward the staircase, and I sat down on the couch while waiting for her to come back.

"This is a right nasty piece of work," I heard Andrew say when Violet showed him the step. "I can definitely replace that step. I can't make this one safe again, no chance in that."

"I believe I have an extra step or two from the builder in storage, somewhere," Violet said, and about ten minutes later, while Andrew was handily working on the step, she came back into the main room.

"I have an idea about catching the diamond thieves," she told me as she made her way to the computer. "However, at this time, that is all it is: an idea. I need to do some more research before I am certain."

"Sounds good," I said, lying down on the couch. Sunlight streamed in through the window, warming my body, and before I knew it, I'd fallen fast asleep.

When I woke up about an hour later, Biscuit had evidently decided that my warm body made an ideal napping partner, as he was lying in the nook of my arm, on his back, his little eyes closed. I smiled and tried my best not to move so as to not wake him, but a moment later he realized I was awake and woke up himself, looking up at me with curious feline eyes before getting up–rather awkwardly, for a cat–and meowing at me as he made his way to the kitchen.

Evidently my cat had decided it was dinner time.

Before I had time to feed him, though, the doorbell rang. I looked over at Violet, who was typing away at her computer, completely engrossed in what she was doing. I couldn't hear anything coming from the staircase, so I assumed Andrew had fixed the step and gone.

"Do you mind getting the door?" she asked me.

"Sure," I replied, making my way toward it. I looked through the peephole in case the murderer had come back, but it was just DCI Williams. I was reasonably sure he wasn't here to kill Violet. Not this time, anyway.

"Hey, what's up?" I asked as I opened the door for him.

"I wanted to see how you and Violet were getting on," he said.

"Well, I just had a nice hour-long nap, but Violet's at her computer and she at least looks like she's been productive. Better her than me, I guess."

Violet had about fifteen different tabs open on her screen, and she was flipping from one to the other at such a quick pace that I had no idea what she was doing, or even what she was thinking about.

"I can come back at another time, if that suits you better," he said, evidently having noticed the same thing I did.

"That would be good, yes," Violet replied. "Give me another hour. You are welcome to stay here, but do not bother me. I believe that I will have the solution then," she continued.

I smiled at DCI Williams. "Don't you love the warm hospitality you always get here?" I asked, and he laughed. Violet had no reaction; I was pretty sure she'd tuned us both out.

"Well, I just stopped by to see if you'd gotten any closer to figuring out how to catch my criminal, but also to make sure you're all right. After all, the fact that there's a triple murderer after you is definitely at the forefront of my mind. I won't insult Violet by suggesting that we park a squad car out the front, even if just to deter the murderer, as I know she'll refuse it. I'll be back in an hour or so."

"Sounds good," I said with a smile as DCI Williams made his way back toward the door. As I went to close the door behind him, I saw some mail had been dropped into Violet's slot; despite my better instincts, I made my way down the steps and picked it up. Luckily, it wasn't booby trapped or anything, and it was actually addressed to me. I suspected Mrs. Michaels must have found it and dropped it off here for me.

As soon as I saw the letterhead, my mouth dried up. It was from the Imperial College School of Medicine. That had been the first place I'd applied to, and now I had an answer. The envelope was a full-size manila, and a little bit on the thicker side, which was a good sign. It meant it wasn't just a single-page rejection letter.

Still, this was England, where wordiness seemed to be very much appreciated. Maybe it was a ten-page rejection letter.

I felt like a seventeen-year old again, back when I was in high school, applying for pre-med programs here and there, checking the mailbox every afternoon in the hopes that I was going to be accepted to my preferred program.

Of course, it was nearly fifteen years later, and I should have been old enough not to feel the butterflies in my stomach as I took the letter inside. I should have just opened it, like an adult, and read what it said instead of staring at it in fear. But, apparently, I wasn't completely an adult just yet.

I walked into the kitchen and put the letter down on the counter. I fed a complaining Biscuit–DCI Williams' visit had not been appreciated by the cat, as it forced him to wait a further five whole minutes for his dinner–while occasionally giving the letter the side-eye.

Eventually, Biscuit was happily munching on his food and I had no other excuses to put off the opening of the letter. Why was I so opposed to opening it, anyway? Was it because I was afraid of rejection, after having been accepted and almost all the way through medical school back in the States? Was it because I didn't actually want to go?

Either way, I reminded myself, I was being silly. My personal worth didn't lie in whether or not a certain university accepted my application, nor was I required to accept if they did say yes. I'd also have to figure out how many years of schooling I'd have to do here in the UK to be considered a fully-fledged doctor; I assumed the transfer of credits wasn't exactly identical to the United States.

After rationalizing with myself for another ten minutes or so, I finally gave in. I grabbed the envelope off the table and ripped it open, my eyes scanning the page.

Dear Miss Coburn,

We are pleased to accept you into the Imperial College of London School of Medicine...

That was all I needed to read. For now, anyway. I sat down and breathed a sigh of relief. All that worry, just to find out I'd made it. I'd been accepted. I mean, of course I knew I should have been. After all, I'd completed nearly an entire degree in the States. It wasn't like I had no idea what the human body was like. But it was still nice to get that acceptance letter. And now, I knew no matter what I decided, that I had the option of going back to medicine.

I just wasn't completely sure if I wanted to yet.

Picking up my phone from the table, I opened it up and texted Brianne.

Just got accepted by the Imperial College for med school.

Her reply came back before I had a chance to text Jake.

Amazing! Well, apart from the whole ICL thing. Wait for Barts and the London to say yes, so we can be study buddies.

I laughed as I read Brianne's text. To be totally honest, I had long ago decided that if I had a choice between where to go, I would prefer to go to St. Bart's and the London for that exact reason: being able to spend more time with Brianne. Even if our schedules weren't identical, we'd definitely be able to see more of each other that way.

We'll see, they haven't said yes yet. I don't even know if I want to do that.

Of course you want to do it silly, you just don't know it yet, my best friend replied.

Maybe, I texted back.

Either way, celebratory drinks tonight?

Can't, working a case with Violet.

That's right, the girl that was next to you, who was strangled? Some idiot in a cop's uniform came by the other day asking about her. I told him it was a good thing Violet was on the case because he obviously didn't have a hope in hell of solving it.

Haha. Was it DI Carlson?

Yeah, that was him. He got mad at me when I admitted I

let Violet look at Amelia's things, and threatened to charge me. So, I told him that I only let Violet look at the things because she was smart enough to recognize a murder victim when she saw one.

I bet he loved that.

He definitely wasn't happy, that was for sure. Anyway, I gotta run. We're going to have to go out to get drinks to celebrate.

Deal, I replied, smiling as I texted Jake my good news as well. Unfortunately, despite my staring at the phone for a reply, I didn't get one, and a minute later I heard the doorbell ring again. I made my way to the door and found DCI Williams waiting once more.

"I know it hasn't quite been an hour, but frankly I just can't wait any longer. I need to know what Violet has figured out as soon as she knows it."

"Well luckily for you, I have both figured out the identities of two of the three men involved in the murder of Amelia Waters, and I have also implemented a plan to stop all three."

"So, you know who tried to kill us?" I asked hopefully, but Violet shook her head.

"Alas, that is the man whose identity I have not yet figured out. But please, come with me, and I will show you how we are going to stop these men."

CHAPTER 18

*D*CI Williams sat down in the armchair and I lay myself across the couch, with Biscuit jumping up and lying down on my legs. Violet wheeled in a full-size whiteboard from God-knows-where. While I was pretty sure she wouldn't mind, I was honestly a little bit scared of looking through Violet's house. The other day when I looked through the closet trying to find an extra towel I found a full rabbit skeleton. So now I decided that whatever skeletons were in Violet's closets—literally—were going to stay there.

"Now," Violet started, like the professor in front of her students. "The main thing that stuck with me with respects to the previous robbery was simply how much jewellery the robbers left behind. After all, their plan was perfect. They entered, they used the algorithm to discover the code used by the safe, and they left with bags full of diamonds. However, the fact that they left so many diamonds and other jewels was strange. It did not fit. Why go to such a risk if not to capitalize on the reward? And then, this afternoon, the answer came to me: it was a practice run."

"A practice run for what?" DCI Williams asked.

"Wait, wait. If you want the answer, you will let me tell my story in my own time," Violet said, raising a hand. "Now, supposing I am correct, it means that the thieves will be targeting another location, presumably somewhere in London. I would be willing to bet, given the imperfection in the death of Amelia Waters, and the frankly rather sloppy attempt on my own life, and potentially that of Cassie's, that the thieves are running on a tighter schedule than they had originally planned on. Evidently, they anticipated having months to practice after getting the program first from Jeremy, and then from Amir. But, their plans have not gone perfectly, and they are having to speed up their schedule. That is to our advantage."

She took a breath and looked around the room at DCI Williams and me. "And so, we find ourselves needing to answer one important question: what is their eventual target? It must be something valuable, if they were willing to use a simple heist in which they stole tens of thousands of pounds worth of diamonds to be a warm-up attempt. And it must also be a target which uses the same model of safe as at the Oxford Street jeweller. While Cassie was having a nap this afternoon, I made some phone calls. I have determined that there are six local jewellers who use that exact same model of safe. However, none of those six store jewels worth enough in that safe at night to be our target. I would suspect that the eventual safe targeted will contain at least ten million pounds worth of jewels."

"A jeweller wouldn't make sense anyway," I mused. "After all, they could rob a jewellery store anytime. It sounds like you think the robbers are after something more time sensitive."

"*Précisement*," Violet nodded. "So, what is happening this week in London where there would be large amounts of jewellery around?"

I shrugged. To be honest, I had absolutely no idea. I wasn't exactly the type to go out and party every weekend and keep up with what was happening in London. I looked over at DCI Williams, who shook his head slightly.

"I know Wimbledon just ended a month ago?" he offered lamely, and Violet rolled her eyes.

"For two young people living in one of the most exciting cities in the world, you are both incredibly dense when it comes to culture. London Fashion Week is happening this week, the second week of October. The first events are tomorrow night."

"And there will be lots of designers around, with jewels," I nodded.

"Not *just* jewels, either," Violet said. "By digging around, I was able to confirm that at one of the parties, being held at the Ritz hotel, a famous celebrity from China, Xin Wu, and her fiancé Hua Zheng, will be unveiling her engagement ring made specially by DeBeers. I was able to obtain a description of the ring from my source as well: it is a four-carat white diamond, surrounded by fifteen smaller, pink diamond stones, set in platinum. My source was able to tell me that the diamonds alone, separated, would be worth well over four million pounds. On top of that, DeBeers will also be displaying numerous other stones at the party, using the occasion of the engagement party to do some marketing."

I gasped audibly at the figure. "Four million? *Just* for the stones?

"Yes," Violet nodded to me. "It is quite the substantial sum, and exactly why I believe that is the target of the thieves."

"This is excellent," DCI Williams said, sitting forward in his seat. "Finally, we have a lead! So all we have to do is keep an eye on the ring, and make sure it's not stolen."

Violet let a small smile creep onto her face.

"Unfortunately for you, Williams, I am afraid it will not be quite so simple as that. You see, I rather suspect that the thieves have already–how do you say–scoped out the hotel where the party will be held quite significantly. And I imagine that they will continue to do so until the day of the heist, which is to be in two days' time. Wu and Zheng are arriving from China the morning after tomorrow, and the party is that night. Apparently DeBeers is bringing the ring–and a number of other high-value diamonds which they will be displaying at the party–that morning. Which means that the heist will almost certainly occur between eleven in the morning and midnight, when the party begins. If I were a betting woman, I would expect it to happen later that night, perhaps between nine and eleven."

"So, you're thinking any police presence might tip them off."

Violet nodded. "*Oui*, I do. In fact, I do not think it is worth the risk at all. Cassie and I, we will stop the thieves. You will remain a safe distance away so you do not spook the thieves, and when we have caught them, you will be able to arrest them."

"You know that as much as I believe in your abilities, I cannot allow a civilian, let alone two civilians, to perform a high-risk operation like the one you're suggesting."

"Fine. I will do nothing, as far as you know. But you are not to do anything either. You *will* scare them. They are too good to not notice you."

DCI Williams glanced sideways at Violet. "All right. I'll make sure we stay away from the Ritz that night, but I'll be somewhere in the vicinity."

"Excellent. And if I happen to stumble across three thieves and murderers, I will make sure to contact you."

I smiled to myself. So, it looked like Violet and I were going to do this anyway. I wondered what on earth Violet had planned.

DCI Williams stood up. "Is there anything you think I should do in the meantime?"

"Just make sure you stay away from that hotel completely. I would not be surprised if the thieves have it under surveillance; if the leader of the task force dedicated to stopping them is seen inside their place of work for any reason, they may decide it is not worth the risk."

A curt nod from DCI Williams showed he understood. "Please do take care of yourself, Violet," he said as he left. "And you too, Cassie. Don't do anything too rash."

"We will not, do not worry," Violet replied as she walked him to the door.

"Wait," DCI Williams said. "You said at the beginning of this conversation that you know who two of the three thieves are. Who are they?"

Violet smiled. "It would be pointless to tell you right now," she replied. "After all, I have absolutely no evidence implicating any of them in any sort of crime. No jury would convict simply on the basis of my logical conclusions. You will know who they are when I have enough evidence against them to have them jailed for life."

"Fine," DCI Williams sighed. "Have it your way. But please be careful."

"I always am," Violet replied as she closed the door behind the policeman and came back into the study.

"Now, I apologize, Cassie. I am afraid I volunteered you for this job without asking. Are you willing to help me foil one of the largest robberies in English history?"

I grinned. "Absolutely."

CHAPTER 19

*V*iolet spent the rest of the night figuring out a plan on how to foil the robbers. I could hear her at the computer, sometimes texting away, and sometimes making a phone call. When I asked if there was anything I could do, she told me that she had it all in hand, and that I was free to do whatever I wanted. I watched Ocean's Eleven on Netflix–I kind of figured the mood required it–before going to bed. After all, in less than forty-eight hours I was going to help stop a jewel heist. I tried not to think about the fact that I hadn't gotten a reply from Jake yet.

The next day, I decided I was going to put a stop to the slanderous articles about Violet in *The London Post-Tribune*. After all, I had leverage now. I knew about the plagiarising. I had a list of articles from which Keegan Coors had literally translated articles from Greek newspapers and passed the words off as his own. In some articles, it was just a few sentences here and there, in others it was the whole article.

Either way, it was going to stop now. I was going to make sure of that.

The London Post-Tribune had its offices in Central London, just a few steps from King's Cross Station, in a modern steel-and-glass building. I made my way through the revolving doors, past security, and to the third floor. As the elevator doors opened, I found myself in a white, modern space as busy as London itself. At least four different phones were ringing, and the hum of people chatting permeated the space. A receptionist spoke hurriedly into a headset, while jotting down notes at a speed no human hand should be able to move.

I moved slowly toward her, feeling completely out of place. Everything moved so quickly here, and everyone around me looked like they knew exactly what they were doing. Straight away I began to wonder if I was doing the right thing. After all, maybe I'd just be laughed out of these offices.

But no, I knew I had to do this. Otherwise, this paper would just keep spreading lies about Violet.

I made my way toward the receptionist. She looked up at me, without saying anything, and I took my cue.

"I need to see Keegan Coors," I told her in my most authoritative voice.

"Do you have an appointment?"

"No," I said, trying to keep a confident air.

"What is it concerning?"

"Uh, it's private."

The girl's eyebrows rose almost imperceptibly. Evidently she thought I was a source. "Who shall I tell him is here?" she asked, tapping the numbers on the phone that led to her headset.

"Tell him it's a friend of Violet Despuis. Tell him it's about Greek news articles."

I was pretty sure that would get me in. Sure enough, the girl muttered into her headset for a moment, and then pressed a button on her desk, motioning to the clouded white glass door to her right.

"Through there, third office on the left," she told me before going back to her other things.

My heart beat in my chest as I made my way toward the door. This was it. I'd never done anything like this before. I was about to blackmail someone into leaving my friend alone. Would this work? How would he react? Was I even doing the right thing?

That last thought flittered through my brain as I made my way past rows and rows of cubicles and to the third office, where Keegan Coors was stencilled onto a frosted glass window. I stood outside the door and wondered for a minute.

After all, wouldn't it be better if I just told the world what he had done? Keegan Coors was a plagiarist. Was I any better than he was if I used that information to blackmail him into leaving Violet alone?

Before I got a chance to really answer the question

myself, the door opened in front of me and I found myself standing in front of a rather short man with a goatee and about fifteen extra pounds on him.

"Yes?" he asked, annoyance on his face obvious.

"Keegan Coors?" I asked in reply.

"Obviously." This conversation was definitely not off to the best start. "What do you want? I'm a busy man."

"I need to talk to you. In private."

"You're the one who wanted to talk to me about Greek stuff?" he asked, turning and making his way back into his office. I wasn't sure if I was imagining it or not, but I almost felt like his shoulders tensed up a little bit, despite his casual demeanor.

"That's right," I said, entering his office and closing the door behind me. It was tiny; barely bigger than a cubicle, but a little bit more private. There was just room for a desk and two small chairs in front of it.

"Well? What is it?"

"I know you've been plagiarising your works from Greek newspapers."

Keegan looked at me carefully as he sat down. I stayed standing. I wasn't one hundred percent sure why; maybe it was because I figured if I sat down now I wouldn't be able to get back up again.

"You said to the receptionist you're a friend of Violet Despuis?"

"Yes, that's right."

"So, let me guess: she sent one of her little minions

here to threaten me because she's angry that I wrote some stuff about her that she thinks is a bit exaggerated." He leaned casually back in his chair. I *definitely* didn't like this guy.

"No, actually. She has no idea I'm here. In fact, I don't think she even read your article. She glanced at the headline, said it was probably worthless drivel like everything else you've written, and moved on." Ok, so I was exaggerating a little bit, but I figured Coors deserved it. The smirk only fell from his face for a split second.

"Ok, so you're here to try and get me to stop writing stuff about her. Well, let me let you in on a little secret, sweet cheeks: I'm kind of a big deal around here. You see, the owner recognizes me as a bit of a genius when it comes to reporting. Besides, it's not plagiarism if you're translating something someone else wrote. Not that I'll ever admit to doing that in public, but just so you know. You can threaten me all you want, but I'm not going to keel over and stop writing about your little girlfriend just because you think you have something on me. Cromwell will definitely keep me on, no matter what."

Ok, that was it. When I'd walked in here, I wasn't sure what I was going to do. But now, I absolutely knew. I shot Coors my best fake smile.

"Oh I'm sorry, I'm afraid you've completely misunderstood me. I'm not here to threaten you, I'm here to warn you." I leaned forward toward him. "You see, I don't like cheaters. I especially don't like cheaters who use their positions to abuse my friends in public. So, I'm going to ruin you. I'm going to go down the street to The Guardian, and I'm going to show them the articles you wrote, and the articles that you stole from the Greek papers. And trust me, I have a pretty big collection of them. And then we'll see just how much Cromwell wants to back you up. After all, he's only going after Violet because she put his son away for being a piece of murderous trash. Will he really defend you when your reputation is in the toilet? After all, you're not family. That's why I'm here. To tell you that you should be Googling a new career path, and fast. No one in journalism is going to touch you come this time tomorrow."

Coors' face had paled to an almost ghostly white by the time I'd finished. He sneered at me.

"Get out of my office."

"You're welcome," I said in as frigid a tone as I could muster. By the time I left, I was absolutely seething with rage. That man was so pompous, so full of himself, and so absolutely unremorseful about the fact that he had been plagiarising.

I did exactly what I'd threatened to do and walked the few blocks to The Guardian offices, where I spoke to a nice reporter and gave her all the information I had. She thanked me, and I made my way back to Kensington. When I walked in, Violet was drawing on her whiteboard.

"Have you threatened the journalist, then?" Violet asked me when I walked in, and I stopped and did a double take.

"Do I talk in my sleep, or something?"

Violet turned and grinned at me. "You cannot after all of this time think that my methods require your subconscious to reveal your secrets in your sleep, do you not? First of all, I know that you were angry about the articles that were written about me and about our investigation. Then, we had breakfast with Charles Dartmouth, a man who deals in secrets, whose company is currently attempting a takeover of *The London Post-Tribune* and who would love to see its value plummet for his own reasons. Afterwards, you come to me and ask for a man who speaks Greek–I have known of the plagiarism of Keegan Coors for a very long time. Evidently Charles gave you enough information for you to uncover it on your own as well. And now this morning you left, and you were obviously pre-occupied; you did not so much as complain about the fact that I put chia seeds in the smoothies I made for breakfast."

"So that's what the gross taste was," I said, scrunching up my nose.

"Those are called vitamins," Violet replied with a smile. "Anyway, I presumed that you have been to *The London Post-Tribune* and that you have threatened Keegan Coors with exposure if he does not leave me alone. Which I must say, while I personally do not care for his writing, I do admire the loyalty of your friendship."

I shot Violet a wry smile. "Unfortunately for you, I'm not *that* good of a friend. That had been my initial plan, and then I wondered if I was being selfish by hiding the fact that one of England's best up-and-coming reporters was absolutely cheating his way up the ranks. Then when I finally met him, he was such an abhorrent human being that I went over to The Guardian and gave them all the information I had. We'll see what comes of it."

Violet burst out laughing. "That is wonderful! Really, I am far happier that you have exposed that cretin than simply using the plagiarism as blackmail. He is scum, that man. Charles will be happy as well."

"Why didn't Charles just go to the paper himself?" I asked. "I mean, don't papers have to protect their sources?"

"Yes, but for a man like Charles, that is still too much of a risk. Sometimes these things become known all the same, and for a man in his position, he cannot be seen as the type of person who speaks of the things he knows. And so, he needed you to do it, so as to make it impossible that anyone could ever trace the source of the information back to him. I suspect he also did not tell you directly what it was to look for?"

"No," I said, shaking my head. "He just told me to look into Keegan Coors' writing, and to look globally. I actually stumbled upon the plagiarism by accident, I thought Bergen Gruppe or The London Bank of Commerce were paying him off."

"Ah, that is also an idea, that. I admire the way you think, and that you got to the truth in the end, accidental or not. You have the makings of a detective in you yet."

"Thanks," I laughed. "Although I'm not sure that's on the table for me. I got accepted to the Imperial College of London yesterday."

"Ah, *mais félicitations!* That is wonderful news!" Violet said, taking me into a hug. "Whether or not you decide to accept, I am glad that you went through with the application and that you now have options."

"Yeah, me too," I smiled. "Now, show me how we're going to stop three thieves tomorrow."

CHAPTER 20

I ended up getting a reply from Jake later that night.

That's amazing news! I'm sorry I didn't get this text earlier, my phone died and I didn't notice. Congratulations!

I felt my heart warm at his words, but I couldn't help but wonder if his excuse was perfectly real. After all, it felt like Jake had been a bit distant for the last few days. Was he ignoring me on purpose? Surely not. Was there another woman? No. Absolutely not. I refused to think that way. I was just being crazy and overly paranoid. There was literally no evidence of anything being wrong, we just kept missing each other over the last few days. Still, I couldn't stop that nagging feeling, no matter how much I knew it was ridiculous.

Thanks. I'm not sure if I'm going to accept, but it's good to have the options.

Absolutely, came Jake's reply a moment later. *Hey, how's your case going?*

Good, we should be finished by tomorrow night. We're going to try and stop a robbery in progress at the Ritz.

I thought you were solving a murder?

It turns out the murderer is one of the Terrible Trio that's been all over the news.

No kidding? Well, listen, I want to hear all about it. Can you clear your weekend? I feel like we need to catch up.

Sure, I replied, my heart constricting slightly. I knew that Jake probably legitimately did want to just have dinner and catch up on my case, but I couldn't help that nagging feeling deep down that told me that he was going to break up with me at last. *I have to go. Big day today*, I replied.

Stay safe! Jake texted back as I put my phone away and sighed. I knew I was being irrational. I knew that listening to that little voice in my head that always thought the worst of everything wasn't a good idea. But I just couldn't help it.

Still, today was way too important a day to dwell on my relationship with Jake and whether it was coming to an end. After all, in less than twelve hours, Violet and I were going to be stopping a major heist committed by three men, one of whom was a likely murderer.

"I have invited an outside consultant to join us today," Violet said with a smile as I heard a knock on the door. "Ah, there she is now."

I wasn't the least bit surprised to see Mrs. Michaels saunter into the room, wearing a pastel purple velour tracksuit, looking bright and chirpy this morning.

"Violet! Cassie! Thank you so much for inviting me to help with your plan," she said as she plopped herself down on the couch, immediately making herself at home. "It has been way too long since I have been involved in this sort of thing but I will endeavor to do my best."

Violet and I both shared a smile.

~

*F*our hours later Violet had outlined her plan, and then we'd gone through it in great detail. Mrs. Michaels had given her input, and had decided that she was going to come along as well, as a guest of the hotel.

"One thing I don't understand," I asked, "is why do the robbers need the algorithm at all? After all, the only reason they couldn't get the night time code from Simon was because he never looked at it. But who's to say that's the case at the Ritz as well?"

Violet nodded. "It is a good question, that, and one that I have asked the manager myself. Because the safe is not meant to be accessed during night hours except in the case of an emergency, their setup is slightly different. The morning codes are sent to the phone of the manager, which presumably the robbers are able to access. However, the evening codes, which are sent at six pm, are sent to a phone kept in a secret location, known only to the manager, locked, and never accessed unless absolutely necessary. Tonight, it will be necessary to access it, since the diamonds and the ring will be needed for the party, but by the time the night manager has done so, it will be too late for the thieves as it means that they will be ready to move the diamonds, along with the armed guards, to the party."

I nodded my understanding. That made sense. If they had half the codes, they could use the algorithm to work out the other half themselves, when the safe would be kept safest as it would be assumed no one had the code.

"Right. First things first, you two ladies need to get into your disguises," Mrs. Michaels said when it was time for us to get ready. It was nearly two in the afternoon, and we expected the theft to happen between nine and eleven. Mrs. Michaels agreed with us that would be the most likely time for the thieves to strike.

Violet went upstairs for a minute, and then came down with a large box filled with wigs. She settled on a short, sandy-blonde wig that was quite a bit lighter than her natural hair color, but still seemed to suit her. I went with a shoulder-length chestnut-brown wig. When I finished tucking my hair and adjusting it, I was amazed at how different I looked with just the change in my hair style and color.

"That is a good color on you," Violet said approvingly. "Now we need the makeup, and then I went and got our uniforms from the Ritz yesterday."

Violet's plan involved us pretending to be employees at the hotel. She had a long conversation the day before with the manager of the hotel, who was in on our plan and fully on board with it. After all, the hotel didn't want anything happening to the jewellery in their vault either. All the press that had occurred after Kim Kardashian had been robbed in Paris a few years ago would be nothing compared to this, if the robbery was successful.

She came back down again a minute later with two suit bags and a box of makeup. Mrs. Michaels watched with interest as Violet began by handing me a box of contact lenses.

"Go into the bathroom and put these in," she ordered. I looked at the box awkwardly.

"Um, I've never actually *put* a pair of contact lenses in before," I said, laughing nervously. "Is it hard?"

"Really?" Violet asked, looking surprised. "Well, it is quite simple, yes. Put the lens on your index finger, hold your eyelids open with your middle fingers, and gently place the lens on your eye. When it is on, remove your finger gently, then blink a couple of times. There are a number of videos on YouTube that can help as well."

"Ok, I might go have a look at those," I said, taking my phone with me as I made my way upstairs to the bathroom. After a few false starts I managed to get the lens in my eye, and tried not to focus on how icky it felt. What if the lens rolled all the way into the back of my eye and got stuck there? I knew that wasn't going to happen. After all, I knew about the anatomy of the eye, and I knew it was actually impossible for a contact lens to get stuck in the back of my eye. Even the odds of it getting stuck under my eyelid were impossibly low. Still, apparently my brain decided today was a good day to panic about things that weren't going to happen.

Looking in the mirror, my eyes had gone from blue to brown, and wow did it stand out. I looked completely different already! If I walked past myself in the street I was pretty sure I wouldn't recognize myself now.

Once Violet had done my makeup, I really didn't recognize myself at all. Or her, for that matter. There was absolutely no way any of the three men would recognize us if they saw us now, unless they looked at us closely.

Mrs. Michaels left first, since she had absolutely no need for a disguise. She was simply playing the role of the lonely old widow who decided to spend a bit of time in the city, away from her garden and away from the drama of her knitting group.

Violet and I walked to Gloucester Street Station and hopped on a train for the four stations to Green Park Station, just outside the Ritz Hotel.

I felt like I was in an Agatha Christie novel as I

looked up and saw the round, thirties-style bulbs advertising the Ritz Hotel, the Ritz Restaurant and the Ritz Club. The building behind it was grand, with alternating flags with the Ritz logo and the Union Jack flying over the street. Everything about it exuded class, but I was torn from my reverie when Violet grabbed my arm.

"Come, you are an employee, you are not supposed to gape at your place of work," she chided me.

"Sorry," I muttered as we made our way around the side of the building toward the back entrance.

"Now, before we go in, I was thinking that your American accent might be a bit of a giveaway, even in London. Can you do an English accent yet?"

"Roight, well, Oi shore can troi," I offered up, and I noticed even Violet struggling not to laugh.

"All right, so definitely not that accent, then," she said.

"Hey, it wasn't that bad," I protested.

"I mean no offense by this, but yes, it was that bad," Violet replied. "Perhaps sticking with your American accent is the safest course of action after all. I recommend studying the English accent in the future, it is useful to be able to swap your voice at will."

"Fine," I muttered as we entered through a service entrance and into the busy kitchen at the back of the hotel. Waiters dressed in finery similar to mine and Violet's moved briskly around while cooks threw out orders, the sound of raw food hitting hot pans sending sizzles through the air while delicious aromas wafted toward us.

"The manager will be meeting us here," Violet said, motioning for me to follow her. We entered a large walk-in pantry on the other side of the kitchen, which was lined with truffle oil imported from Italy, Dijon mustard from France and a ton of other stuff that looked like it belonged on the shelves of one of those high-end delis where the BLTs cost fifteen bucks and were made with prosciutto instead of bacon.

"Try not to eat anything you haven't been invited to eat," Violet told me as she saw me eyeing the stores on the shelves, and I stuck my tongue out at her.

"Why are we meeting in here?" I asked.

"Well, I suspect that our thieves have likely got rather extensive camera coverage in the parts of the hotel which they find relevant to their plan. As I do not know their plan, I think it would be better if we are safe, rather than sorry. If we are spotted, or even if something out of the usual is noticed today on their cameras, I suspect that they will abandon their plan. Without catching them in the act, it will make the murder of Amelia Waters much more difficult to solve, and we will have no leverage to threaten them with even if we do solve it."

Just then, the door opened and a woman dressed in a smart business suit, her brown hair tied back in a tight bun, walked in. She was obviously all business.

"Miss Despuis, Miss Coburn," she said, shaking

both our hands. Evidently my presence here had already been described to her.

"This is Mrs. Evangeline Edgeware, the manager here at the Ritz," Violet explained to me. "The house safe, where the jewels are currently located, is inside her office."

"Yes," Evangeline nodded. "I have copied the keys required to enter, and Violet, I have found for you and emailed to you the copy of the building's HVAC systems that you asked for. One of those keyrings also has a key that works on all of the guest room doors. You are welcome to use room 131, which is just down the hall from my office, as your headquarters of sorts. It is the room that has been assigned to your associate Mrs. Michaels."

"Thank you," Violet said, taking the two keys and handing the one with multiple keys on it to me. It wasn't like one of the standard electronic room keys you get at most hotels these days, this one was the kind you still physically put into a lock. The key itself was gold, on an oval-shaped key ring, navy blue in color, with the Ritz logo printed on the front, and trimmed in gold as well. I slipped it into the pocket of my uniform.

"I've got the details about the security from DeBeers," Evangeline continued. "There are three men posted in the hotel–one is at the bar, one is in the lobby and will dart in and out, and the other is a registered guest, who are all plain clothes. They are DeBeers private security, all ex-Special Forces. They are aware that you are here, and they are aware of the potential threat, but they are also very well trained. I'm assured that they won't do anything rash or stupid."

"Spoken like someone who has never dealt with this country's supposed "special" forces," Violet muttered. "Well, if we have any luck, they will not immediately give themselves away. Besides, I am certain that the robbers will be expecting such heavy security."

"I'll be leaving at six, just as I always do," Evangeline told us. "Please keep me updated on what happens. There is a night manager, but she has a different office."

"We will, thank you," Violet said, and with a brisk nod, Evangeline Edgeware left the room.

"Now," Violet told me. "It is just after five in the afternoon. Let us get ready, shall we?"

CHAPTER 21

My heart raced as Violet talked me through the plan once more.

"Now that we have the schematics, let us have a look," Violet said, opening up her email on her phone. Sure enough, there was an email there from Evangeline, with a PDF attachment. It was a blueprint of the building, which showed the HVAC system as well.

"You're really going to climb through the ducts of the building to get to the manager's office?" I asked, still kind of amazed that this was Violet's plan.

"Yes," she nodded. "I suspect that the men will be coming through the main door, but in case they are not, I want to have eyes inside the room. Seeing as we cannot risk that the men have a camera inside the room and would see us enter, that means that I will go through the ducts and look that way, while you will keep an eye out on the main hallway from room 131."

"All right, let's get going then," I said. "Do you have the small camera for me?"

"I do," Violet replied. "Do you remember my instructions on how to get to the laundry room from here?"

"I do."

"Good. Then turn your phone to vibrate only. Only text when absolutely necessary. Mrs. Michaels will be around as well if we need her."

"Good luck," I told Violet.

"We do not need luck, we have this planned to perfection," came her reply, and I smiled to myself as I left the pantry and made my way back into the kitchen.

I tried to look as normal as possible as I made my way through to the laundry room. Reaching into my pocket, I saw the tiny camera Violet had given me. She told me that she'd gotten the idea from the robbers themselves, with the way they used the camera to get the numbers generated from the safe.

I grabbed a pile of clean towels and made my way back up to the ground floor, passing by the manager's office on the way.

With the camera—a simple dot, barely bigger than a pin head—in my finger, I made my way along the plush red, blue and white floral-printed fabric and past white flowers in Greek-style vases and olden-style golden lights. I stopped at one of the vases, pretending to notice a smudge on it, and wiped it away while secretly placing the camera, with its sticky backing, on one of the leaves of the flowers. I had it set up so the camera looked past the Enquiries Desk and toward the manager's office: if anyone came this way, I'd be able to see them on live video.

I continued down the hall, making a concerted effort to avoid looking at the manager's office. Instead, I continued down to room 131 and knocked on the door. "Housekeeping," I called out, resisting the urge to use my apparently terrible English accent.

I waited a moment and then took my key from my pocket and put it into the lock. Luckily, I guessed the right key correctly on the first try and the room swung open. I placed the towels down on the plush bed and looked around. It felt like I'd stepped back in time in the best way. The white walls trimmed with gold looked like they could have been those of the walls of Versailles, while an antique-style cabinet held a modern touch—the flat-screen TV—next to the marble mantle over which sat a large mirror. If the reason we were here wasn't so serious, I could have very easily pretended I was in Downton Abbey for a little while. Mrs. Michaels wasn't here, which didn't surprise me at all. She was without a doubt in the Palm Court, taking part in the five-thirty sitting of afternoon tea.

Mrs. Michaels' job was to be on the lookout for anything suspicious. Violet was completely certain that the men wouldn't show their faces inside the hotel, and that they would be either wearing heavy makeup as the two of us were doing, or masked completely. But with her extensive knowledge of crime and how it worked, Mrs. Michaels was the perfect gatekeeper for us, the first person to notice if there was someone in the vicinity acting suspiciously.

She had left my iPad on the bed, where I had asked her to, and I immediately connected to the WiFi and opened up the link Violet had emailed me, which opened up a video feed that showed the door of the Manager's office. The fisheye view of the camera also gave me a good look down the entrance hall that led in from Davies Street. This way, two of the three entrances were covered, and if by chance the thieves did make it into the room without either myself or Mrs. Michaels noticing, Violet was in the air ducts and could tell us all the same that they were breaking in.

Just then, my phone buzzed on the bed next to me. It was a text from Violet.

Am in place. Looking through the duct at the manager's office now.

My heart skipped a beat as I read Violet's text. That meant that with me in this room, looking at the video feed, and Mrs. Michaels having her afternoon tea, the three of us were in place, and we had only to wait until the thieves decided to strike.

Whenever you watch a movie, it never shows the hours that pass during a stakeout. They always show the cops sitting in their car, and then maybe one of them goes to get a coffee or something, and bam! Bad guys. They don't show the heart-pounding adrenaline at the beginning of the stakeout, but more importantly, they also don't show the multiple hours in the middle when the adrenaline wears off and boredom kicks in.

I mean, it wasn't like I was ready to go home or anything. After all, I knew that at any given moment the three thieves, three of the most wanted men in England, one of whom had successfully killed three people and almost killed Violet and me, could come into this hotel and try to steal millions of pounds worth of diamonds and jewellery. But still, there was only so much staring at a screen and watching nothing happen that I could do without feeling a *little* bit bored.

I eventually turned on the TV and watched an old episode of Top Gear while still keeping an eye on the iPad. Though to be honest, I had no real idea what was going on in the TV show. As much as I was bored watching the iPad, the stakes were still so high I couldn't really concentrate on anything else. At about eight, Mrs. Michaels came into the room. She was dressed like the Queen, complete with a fancy hat and a cute square handbag on her arm.

"Afternoon Tea has long since finished, I'm afraid," she told me. "I saw no sign of anything out of the ordinary. I received Violet's text that she's in the air duct. That girl, always willing to go the extra mile to find a criminal. Well, if it's all the same to you, I think I'll retire to one of the main areas. I'll continue to keep an eye out for anything suspicious, and let you know if anything were to turn up. Please do let me know if there's anything else I can do."

"Thanks, Mrs. Michaels. I will, for sure. Just keep an eye out, ok?"

"Of course," she replied. "See you later," she said with a wink as she left the room. For a woman of her age, Mrs. Michaels was incredibly spry. I'd be happy if I still managed to be that active in my fifties, let alone my eighties.

I smiled to myself and turned back to the iPad to make sure I hadn't missed anything important during the two-minute conversation with Mrs. Michaels. Luckily for me, everything was going on just as usual. I was fairly certain the man in front of the advice counter had been playing Solitaire for most of the last hour.

By the time nine-thirty came around, I knew we were in prime time for when Violet thought the theft was most likely to happen, but I was also *bored*. I'd now been sitting in this room and watching the iPad for almost four hours. I was so bored I'd just finished trying–and failing–to do a push-up!

Thinking that maybe I should go to the gym, in case I ever needed to lift something heavier than a shopping bag, my phone buzzed next to me. I grabbed it in excitement. Had Mrs. Michaels spotted something? No, it was from Violet.

I believe the men are coming in through the air duct I am currently in. Come and get me!

I went from pure boredom to outright panic in under a second. Leaping from the bed, I double checked that the keys were in my pocket as I sprinted out of the room and down a floor to the manager's office. If the men were in the duct, that meant they probably weren't looking at any cameras anyway, and besides, making sure Violet wasn't caught was more important than anything else.

I fumbled with the keys for a minute before managing to enter the manager's office and quickly turning on the flashlight on my phone. I didn't want to turn the lights on completely lest the light make it to the men and they realize something was wrong.

"Here," I heard Violet hiss as soon as I entered. I looked to where the sound was coming from, to my left, and saw a standard air duct leading into the room. The hole was about a foot and a half high, and it was covered with a side table to hide the duct. I grabbed the side table and moved it, then looked at the screws. Flat heads. That was good.

"One second," I whispered to Violet, moving to the manager's desk. I scanned the dark mahogany for a second before finding what I was after: an ivory letter opener with a golden hilt. Ok, it was a lot fancier than what I was looking for, but it would work.

"I can hear them coming," Violet whispered as I began to work. I used the letter opener, which was a lot sharper than I expected, as a screwdriver, doing my best to undo the screws as quickly as I could. It felt like every turn took an eternity, and my heart beat faster with every turn, but eventually I got all four screws out and I moved the grate off the wall as quietly as I could before offering Violet a hand. I pulled her out and she fell to the floor, helping me put the grate back.

"Leave the screws a little bit loose," Violet whispered to me, and I nodded my understanding. A moment later she grabbed me, and I just had time to put the letter opener back on the desk as Violet ran me toward the closed curtain and shoved us both behind it. I turned off the flashlight on my phone as I heard the first voice of one of the men.

"Christ, this is a bit of a tight fit," I heard one voice say. I frowned; something about it seemed familiar.

"Almost there," I heard another voice reply, this one with a bit of an accent. I looked down at our feet; luckily the curtain was one of those fancy floor-to-ceiling types, and we were completely covered.

Suddenly, the sound of the grate hitting the floor resonated through the room and I took a deep breath. This was it. We were going to catch some robbers.

CHAPTER 22

 didn't even dare peek through the curtains. The men turned on the lights and I looked over at Violet, whose eyes were closed as she listened closely to what was happening in the room.

"There, behind the painting," the first man said, and there was a small thud a moment later as presumably the men removed the painting that had been covering the safe.

"Do you have the code?" the man with the accent asked. I heard the sound of a few beeps—maybe six or seven—and then a latch opening. Violet grabbed me by the wrist; I knew our time to strike was near. I put my hand into my pocket and grabbed the Taser Violet had given me earlier, along with a lesson in its use.

"Is it there?" a third voice asked.

"It's all here. Let's grab it, and then get out of here. The three security men are still in the lobby, so no panicking. We just calmly walk out of here, and walk to the car. We practiced this. This is why we're all wearing the makeup; we won't get caught."

"Right," one of the men replied. I could hear the tinkle of jewels being shoved into a bag. Violet nodded at me. This was our cue.

Violet and I burst out of the curtain. I liked to imagine that we looked like Batman and Robin, bursting onto the scene dramatically and striking a pose, but in reality I got a little bit stuck in the curtain and began flailing about with my hands until finally I sprung out of the curtain myself and faced the three men.

We each had our Tasers levelled at the men, and my mouth dropped in shock when I saw them. The man in the middle I didn't recognize. He was on the shorter side, with dark hair and a thin mustache. Oxford professor Alan Knightly and Oliver Hollingsworth, Amelia Waters' ex-boyfriend and one of the most powerful men in England. No wonder I recognized the voice. The three men wore wigs and makeup, same as Violet and I, but they were still recognizable under-neath–though security camera footage would defi-nitely struggle to make out the details that allowed us to recognize them.

"Stop," Violet ordered. "You have been caught, and you are going to jail."

"I told you we should have made more of an effort to kill her," Knightly said to the man in the middle.

"I couldn't make it look like an accident, there was no more time. It would have been too suspicious, too many questions asked."

"Well this isn't better," Hollingsworth said from the other side of the man. "How the hell did you know we were going to be here, anyway?" he asked, moving toward the desk.

"Do not move another inch," Violet ordered, levelling her Taser toward him. Her hand was rock steady, whereas I felt like I was going to faint at any minute. I wasn't exactly used to threatening murderers. "I have known the three of you, Knightly, Hollingsworth and the man known as *"Il Fissatore"* were the thieves for days. Now, the police are waiting outside to take you in."

"She's bluffing," Hollingsworth laughed, but the other two men began to look a bit nervous. Knightly was holding a Louis Vuitton messenger bag from which I saw the sparkle of diamonds; he clutched it so hard his knuckles were white from the effort. Evidently Hollingsworth was the one of the three who wasn't the least bit worried by our arrival. Not outwardly, anyway. "I recommend you put those weapons down and leave now," Hollingsworth continued. "Before things get ugly for you."

Violet smiled. "It is adorable, that you believe you will get out of here with the profits of your thefts, and that you will get away with them."

"Oh, but I will," Hollingsworth said, suddenly

flinging the letter opener that I'd left on the desk toward Violet. She ducked down to avoid it, but not fast enough. Rather than getting her in the heart, the letter opener went straight through Violet's shoulder, causing her to yelp out in pain as she dropped the Taser.

For a split second, it was like everything was completely still. Then, chaos. I immediately unclipped the safety on the Taser and shot it at Knightly, who let out a cry and went down like a shot and stayed down, his body twitching. I didn't even realize I was doing it; it was almost a reflex.

Il Fissatore grabbed the messenger bag which had fallen from Knightly's hands and ran to the door at top speed; he was making a run for it. He threw the door open and ran out.

At the same time, Hollingsworth lunged toward the door as well, but he wasn't as agile as the other man; before he got there, Violet let out a grunt as she threw out a leg, the dagger still sticking out of her shoulder. Hollingsworth cried with surprise as he lost his balance, falling to the floor. I ran over to Knightly to make sure he was well and truly out; it seemed the Taser's electric charge had knocked him unconscious.

Meanwhile, Hollingsworth groaned as he got up, and lunged at Violet. She spun around and roundhouse kicked him in the face, making the man collapse to the ground. He too was unconscious.

"Text Williams," Violet ordered to me, her voice

surprisingly steady given that she'd been stabbed in the shoulder and had still managed to subdue a man completely. "Tell him *Il Fissatore* has escaped."

"I wouldn't be too sure about that," a familiar voice said from outside the room. Mrs. Michaels popped her head in, still wearing her Sunday best. Violet and I made our way to her and looked outside; a couple of workers were trying to hold back the small crowd that was now gathering around the area where the man who had run out with the diamond was now lying, unconscious, on the ground. I gaped at Mrs. Michaels.

"Did you do that?" I asked.

"Dear, I keep telling you, I'm old, not useless."

"I know. I know that. But still…. How?"

Mrs. Michaels opened up her handbag and winked as she showed me what was inside. Whereas normal old ladies kept–I assumed–little packets of tissues and coin purses in their handbags, Mrs. Michaels had a full-on brick in hers. No wonder the man was unconscious.

"I saw you running past at top speed into the office and assumed it was going down, so I waited out the front here just in case I was needed. When I saw this man run past clutching a bag, I assumed he wasn't up to anything good, so I hit him in the face with the bag as he came past."

Violet laughed. "And that, Mrs. Michaels, is why I invited you to come along."

"Madam, I'm calling an ambulance, and the police," one of the workers said to Violet. "Are you all right?"

"Oh it is fine, it is not the first time I have been stabbed, and it will likely not be the last," Violet said, waving him away. "Besides, the police are coming, DCI Williams is on his way now."

"Ok, well, this might not be the first time you've been stabbed, but that doesn't mean you don't need medical attention," I complained. "Please *do* call that ambulance," I told the man, earning myself a glare from Violet, but even she knew that with blood pouring from the wound, she was going to need professional attention. "And get me some clean towels," I ordered as I moved Violet toward a nearby chair. Mrs. Michaels picked up the bag of diamonds; I figured it was safe with her. I winced as I looked at the antique-looking chair I sat Violet down on, knowing that the upholstery would likely be ruined by blood in a few minutes.

I did my best to stem the flow of blood from the wound, making sure not to remove the letter opener from Violet's shoulder until the ambulance arrived. The three security men hired by DeBeers came by just afterwards.

"What's going on here?"

"Step away from that office!"

"Arrest that woman!"

It was complete chaos. Violet, despite my insistence that she stay seated, stood up, her eyes flashing in anger.

"*This woman*, as you so crudely refer to me, is the only reason any of you will still have a job tomorrow, so I suggest you treat me with a little bit more respect."

"It's Violet Despuis, the detective," I heard one of the men hiss to the other.

"Oh yeah? Why's that? What happened here?" the third man asked.

"An attempted theft of the diamond ring whose security you were entrusted with is what occurred," Violet replied. "Luckily for you, and for everyone involved, I am by far the superior investigator in this room, and I was able to foil the heist with the help of my friends."

"So where are the diamonds?" one of the men asked.

"My associate has taken them for safekeeping, until the police can retrieve them. No doubt they will be used as evidence in the trials for burglary and for murder."

"Murder?" one of the men asked.

"Yes, murder. As I said, my detective skills are far superior to yours, and I do not have the patience to explain to you the history of these three men."

One of the men looked like he was going to protest, but just then DCI Williams walked in, followed by a half dozen other uniformed police.

"Violet! Are you all right?" he asked.

"Obviously I am all right, there are three men here for you to arrest, which is far more important than asking after me," she scolded at him.

"All right, it's time for you to sit down and stop annoying people," I ordered. "You need to relax, decreasing your blood pressure is paramount right now."

Violet grumbled something I couldn't quite make out, but the logic of my words crept in and she sat down on the chair once more until the ambulance arrived. I handed her over to the EMTs, who immediately loaded her up in the ambulance.

"I'm going with Violet," I told DCI Williams, who watched as Hollingsworth, the last of the men, was led away in cuffs. "We have the diamonds, I'll make sure Violet gets them to you."

"Tell her thanks from me," he said. "And that I hope she recovers well. And thank you, as well."

"Sure, will do. And no problem. It was actually kind of fun," I replied. It was, really. I mean, other than the four or so hours where I was bored out of my skull, and the part where there was a full-on standoff. And of course, the part where Violet was stabbed.

So really, very little of it was fun. But the adrenaline was pumping, and if I had to do it all over again, I knew I would.

I hopped into the back of the ambulance, the EMTs pulled the doors closed behind me, and we sped off, sirens blaring, to the nearest hospital.

CHAPTER 23

I had never been to Guy's and St. Thomas' Hospital, on the south side of the Thames before. I had seen the inside of more of London's Accident and Emergency wards than I ever thought I would when I moved here. Violet was seen almost immediately, and after applying local anesthetic the doctor removed the letter opener and stemmed the bleeding, thanks to the help of numerous stitches. The whole thing took a few hours, since it took a very long time to stop the bleeding from such a large wound after the letter opener was removed, and by the time Violet was finally given the all-clear to go home–along with a sling to stop her from moving her left arm for a few weeks while the wound healed–it was nearly three in the morning.

"Thank you for coming to the hospital with me," Violet said as we left the Accident and Emergency ward. She began to take off the sling, but I put my hand on it.

"What on earth do you think you're doing?"

"I am not wearing this, it is impeding with the necessary use of my arm."

"You know what else will impede the use of that arm? You bleeding to death when that wound re-opens because you wouldn't listen to the doctor. You're keeping it on."

"I am not wearing this for three weeks."

"Fine, but you're at least wearing it for a few days until the skin has a little bit of time to heal."

"You are *such* a doctor."

"That's right, I am, so listen to what I say when you get stabbed in the shoulder."

As we drove home, I couldn't wait to pass out in my bed–well, Violet's guest bed–and go to sleep.

"We will go see Mrs. Michaels in the morning," Violet told me. "I suspect she will be waiting for us for morning tea."

"As long as it's not before ten," I replied as the cab pulled up to the curb. The two of us made our way inside, and true to form, I fell asleep pretty much straight away.

Waking up at nine, I made my way down to the study and found myself pleasantly surprised at the fact that Violet was still wearing her sling. I got dressed and had a hot shower to wake myself up, then we went across the street to Mrs. Michaels' house.

"Come in!" she shouted when I rang the bell, and Violet and I opened the unlocked front door and made our way upstairs.

As soon as we made our way up to Mrs. Michaels' living room I burst out laughing. Our hostess was wearing the same pastel purple velour tracksuit she wore to Violet's place the other day, but this time, she had accessories, in the form of *all* the jewellery that was taken from the hotel safe the night before. The light glistened off all the stones, including the huge diamond ring which Mrs. Michaels proudly sported on her ring finger.

"Welcome, ladies, welcome!" she said, her voice as bright as the jewels. "I'm so glad you could make it! Please, have a seat, I'll bring the tea out in just a moment."

I stood where I was, enjoying the scene for just a moment. It was like someone had dumped Mrs. Michaels in glitter. She returned a moment later with a platter of tea, liberally decorated with a few loose stones, and I laughed as Violet and I sat down and each accepted a cup.

"You do realize that you will need to return these jewels," Violet told Mrs. Michaels when we'd sat down. "After all, the police will require them as evidence."

"What, oh these little things? Why, they're just part of my collection. I've had these for years!" Mrs. Michaels replied with a cheeky grin.

"I am serious, I need to give these to DCI Williams."

"Oh I know dear, but just let me have a bit more fun with them for just a couple of hours. It's been so long since I've seen the spoils of a good heist."

"Ah, but this was not a good heist. At least, it would have been, if not for the fact that I knew they were going to be there."

"Yeah, about that," I interrupted. "You *knew* that it was Knightly and Hollingsworth, didn't you?"

"I did," Violet admitted. "Insofar as one can be certain of anything with absolutely no proof, at any rate."

"But how?" I asked. "How did you know who the three men were?"

"First, there was the fact that there could not have been very many people in the world who knew of the algorithm. As soon as it became obvious that the algorithm was the key to finding the identity of the killer, and that our killer was one of the Terrible Trio, our suspect pool became very limited. Yes, one of the others could have told someone indiscreetly about it, but did you notice the painting hanging on the wall of Professor Knightly's office?"

"Yeah, that thing with the lilies."

Violet cracked a small smile. "That 'thing with the lilies', as you so eloquently put it, is a Monet painting that was sold anonymously two months ago for three million pounds. Our professor was investing in art worth far in excess of what his annual salary would allow."

"Maybe it was a print?" I shrugged, but Violet shook her head.

"I knew at once it was not. It is the real deal. Art is not only a good investment, but also an excellent manner to launder the stolen diamonds. I am certain that he told his friends and coworkers that it was a forgery, that he simply enjoyed the art for what it was, but he was lying. It is in fact the real McCoy, as you say in English. Also, I thought it suspicious that Knightly gave us no details about the algorithm project at the time. Normally, when speaking about one's passion, one does so liberally, giving out too much information rather than too little."

"Ok, but what about Hollingsworth? Was it the earrings?" I asked.

"No, not the earrings. As you will remember, the earrings he gave Amelia Waters were made of sapphire, not diamond. The Terrible Trio only ever stole diamonds. But do you remember the two small stones you found in Amelia's jacket?"

"Yeah, I do."

"Well, they were not simple pebbles. They were, in fact, uncut diamonds."

My mouth dropped open. "Really?"

Mrs. Michael laughed gently. "But of course, dear. Everyone always assumes that diamonds come out of the ground shiny and bright, but in fact, they're rather unimpressive until they've been polished. To an untrained eye, they just look like, well, pebbles."

"Well that's disappointing," I said. "Why didn't you say anything at the time?"

Violet shrugged. "What was there to say? To be totally honest, I did not factor in that you would not immediately recognize the diamonds. I at first suspected Amelia might have been involved in the thefts as well, but I soon came to a different conclusion–someone *close to her* had been involved in the thefts, and used her in order to get close to her, and find out about her schedule before killing her and making it look like a suicide. And so that left Oliver Hollingsworth."

"And the third man was the one who actually killed her, right? Because the other two men had really good alibis."

"*Précisement*, and that is what made their plan so ingenious. There were three men, but two were known to the victim. The third, *Il Fissatore*, did not know any of the Oxford students. He had no link to them, no reason to want any of them dead. He was the perfect killer. And in fact, if we had not determined the algorithm's role in the whole affair, it is likely that the case would have gone completely unsolved."

"Who is this *Il Fissatore* anyway?"

"An Italian fellow, his name means 'The Fixer,'" Mrs. Michaels replied. "He's one of the most experienced robbers currently active, and a real jack-of-all-trades. He's never been caught, and never even been identified. In fact, some people even doubted he existed. He's known for striking without leaving any evidence for the police to find. It's rumored that he started off with the Pink Panther gang, but I have my doubts; they were mainly Eastern European, those fellows."

"He was the one who planned the robberies, Hollingsworth was the one who found the information about the targets to hit, and Knightly provided the algorithm for them to be able to enter the safe without problem," Violet said.

"Wow," I said, shaking my head. "Why would they do it though? I mean, Hollingsworth is one of the richest men in England, right?"

"Yes, but no amount of money can make up for a good surge of adrenaline," Violet said. "Hollingsworth was into horse racing, which is where he met Amelia, but I suspect that he simply found life boring. He needed something more exciting, and he found it in the thefts. As for Knightly, I suspect that it was the money which attracted him. I would imagine that Knightly ran into Hollingsworth, who knew *Il Fissatore*, and that is how the three of them got together. We will know for certain when we have their confessions. And on that note, I am afraid, Mrs. Michaels, that I am going to have to ask for the jewellery."

"Oh, you're no fun," Mrs. Michaels said, looking longingly at the diamonds. "I do miss it, you know."

"Perhaps I am not the best person to be admitting your longing for theft to," Violet warned.

"Ah, but you are, dear. You see, if I tell you, I can't

really do anything, can I? Knowing that the great Violet Despuis would come after me is enough to know I wouldn't get away with it, no matter how much I'd like to tell myself otherwise. Now, let me go get you the bag these all came in."

I picked up one of the diamonds off the tray and looked at it closely. It glimmered so nicely in the light, but I couldn't help but think how sad it was that three promising young students had been killed in the attempted theft of a piece of shining rock.

"*All* of the diamonds, please," Violet chastised when Mrs. Michaels had refilled the bag, and she sighed, reaching into a pocket and pulling out a gorgeous bracelet.

"I just wanted a little souvenir, nothing wrong with that," she replied, earning herself a *look* from Violet, and I laughed.

"Fine, then I will pretend I did not see you slip a solitary loose stone underneath your teacup," Violet replied. "That will have to do as a souvenir."

"I knew there was a reason I liked having you as a neighbor," Mrs. Michaels winked. "Please let me know what happens with the confessions, I love being the first to have gossip back in the old circles."

Violet and I left, and I realized with a start that it was Friday! Jake had asked me to clear my weekend, and I wondered if that meant we were going out tonight. I sent him a quick text.

We doing anything tonight?

Making my way back to Violet's, I went back to sleep for a few hours, waking up to a reply from Jake.

No, but I recommend getting up early tomorrow. I'll be there to pick you up at six.

I like pretending 6am isn't a time that exists, but for you, I'll make an exception I replied before making my way back downstairs, to where Biscuit was begging Violet for food as she cooked up an omelette.

"Traitor," I muttered to the cat, giving him a pet as I walked past him.

"Would you like some?" she asked.

"Depends, have you poisoned it?" I replied.

"It has been *days* since that happened, let it go," she replied, and I laughed.

"In that case, yes please."

"I received a call from DCI Williams," Violet said. "Hollingsworth and Knightly admitted to everything, including *Il Fissatore* killing the three students. All three men will be going to jail for a very long time."

I smiled, and Violet continued. "Detective Inspector Carlson is fuming mad, apparently. He claims it vastly unfair that DCI Williams happened to capture the criminals which were supposed to be his."

"Oh well, he'll get over it," I said as Violet put an omelette on my plate. I took a bite and didn't immediately pass out. So far, so good!

*A*t five thirty the next morning I swore as my alarm went off, and I sent Jake a quick text.

Being up this early had better be worth it.

It will be he sent back a minute later, and I smiled. I wondered what it was he had planned.

At two minutes to six a black taxi cab pulled up in front of Violet's house. I got in and found Jake there, dressed in slacks and a t-shirt. Giving him a quick kiss, I looked at him questioningly.

"Why are we doing anything this early? Is anyone even up right now other than City bankers who are hopped up on cocaine and haven't gone to bed yet?"

Jake laughed. "Wow, you're certainly learning what London's all about pretty quickly. But you'll see. I promise, it's going to be worth it. By the way, did you bring your passport?"

Forty minutes later we were standing in front of the

gate at London Heathrow, waiting to board the flight to Rome.

"Are you serious?" I squealed when Jake handed me a boarding pass. He'd refused to tell me where we were going, and as soon as I saw Rome–FCO on the pass, my heart raced with excitement.

"Yeah," he grinned. "A few days ago, I saw a good fare online, so I booked it, but I hadn't actually booked the time off work. That's why my texts have been so spotty lately; I did a whole bunch of overtime to get in the boss' good books, since I was supposed to work today and tomorrow."

All the built-up stress inside of me evaporated immediately. Jake wasn't pulling away. There was no other woman. I'd just been being completely silly while he planned the most incredible surprise for me.

I laughed and leaned into Jake as the stewardess announced that our flight was about to begin boarding.

One of my goals when I'd moved to London was to eventually see a bit more of the world. After all, living in London, I was now only a few hours away from some of the most amazing and famous sights in the world. I'd never quite made the time to do it, though.

Jake was, once again, moving me a bit out of my comfort zone. We ate gelato from a little place called Ciampini, tucked away between the Spanish Steps and the Pantheon, that was hands down the most amazing gelato I'd ever had. We wandered around the Coliseum and the Roman Forum, and walked along the Tigris at night after a meal in a little restaurant in Trastevere where we struggled through the Italian-only menus before asking the waitress to just bring us anything. Of course, it was phenomenal.

After spending the night in a hotel room so tiny it was comical, Jake and I made an early-morning stop at the Trevi Fountain before taking a train back to the airport for our flight back to London.

"This was easily the best weekend of my life," I said to Jake when we landed at Heathrow once more. He turned to me and grinned.

"I'm glad you liked it. And seeing as you just helped capture three of the most wanted criminals in the country, I think you deserve it."

I grinned as we passed a newsagent and I saw the headline: *The London Post-Tribune Embroiled in Plagiarism Scandal.*

Just when I thought my day couldn't get any better.

⁓

*B*ook 5: Cassie's adventures continue in **Stabbed in Shoreditch.** When Violet is hired to prove the innocence of a convicted murderer, Cassie discovers that not only is an innocent man's life at stake, but also that solving a ten-month-old murder has its own unique challenges.

Click or tap here to read Stabbed in Shoreditch now

ALSO BY SAMANTHA SILVER

First of all, I wanted to thank you for reading my book. I well and truly hope you enjoyed reading this book as much as I loved writing it.

If you enjoyed Strangled in Soho I'd really appreciate it if you could take a moment and leave a review for the book to help other readers find it as well.

Other Cassie Coburn Mysteries:

Poison in Paddington (Cassie Coburn Mystery #1)

Bombing in Belgravia (Cassie Coburn Mystery #2)

Whacked in Whitechapel (Cassie Coburn Mystery #3)

Stabbed in Shoreditch (Cassie Coburn Mystery #5)

Killed in King's Cross (Cassie Coburn Mystery #6)

Ruby Bay Mysteries

Death Down Under (Ruby Bay Mystery #1)

Arson in Australia (Ruby Bay Mystery #2)

The Killer Kangaroo (Ruby Bay Mystery #3)

Western Woods Mysteries

Back to Spell One (Western Woods Mystery #1)

Two Peas in a Potion (Western Woods Mystery #2)

Three's a Coven (Western Woods Mystery #3)

Four Leaf Clovers (Western Woods Mystery #4)

Magical Bookshop Mysteries

Alice in Murderland (Magical Bookshop Mystery #1)

Murder on the Oregon Express (Magical Bookshop Mystery #2)

The Very Killer Caterpillar (Magical Bookshop Mystery #3)

Death Quixote (Magical Bookshop Mystery #4)

Pride and Premeditation (Magical Bookshop Mystery #5)

Willow Bay Witches Mysteries

The Purr-fect Crime (Willow Bay Witches #1)

Barking up the Wrong Tree (Willow Bay Witches #2)

Just Horsing Around (Willow Bay Witches #3)

Lipstick on a Pig (Willow Bay Witches #4)

A Grizzly Discovery (Willow Bay Witches #5)

Sleeping with the Fishes (Willow Bay Witches #6)

Get your Ducks in a Row (Willow Bay Witches #7)

Busy as a Beaver (Willow Bay Witches #8)

Moonlight Cove Mysteries

Witching Aint's Easy (Moonlight Cove Mystery #1)

Witching for the Best (Moonlight Cove Mystery #2)

ABOUT THE AUTHOR

Samantha Silver lives in British Columbia, Canada, along with her husband and a little old doggie named Terra. She loves animals, skiing and of course, writing cozy mysteries.